Silence is White

Silence is white

stories, poems & illustrations for
Seb Doubinsky

edited by

Chris Kelso

WEIRDO ⊂∾MAGNET

Silence is White: stories, poems & illustrations for Seb Doubinsky
edited by Chris Kelso

First published in 2017 by
WEIRDO**⌁**MAGNET
an imprint of Leaky Boot Press
http://www.weirdomagnet.com

ISBN: 978-1-909849-52-5

Contents

Introduction

Chris Kelso

Seb Doubinsky is desperate to be an indie writer because at heart he's a punk rocker. He's determined not to sell-out. So far, Seb has successfully kept the angling tendrils of mainstream success at bay—*just*. It's funny, his resistance is something I've come to admire greatly in him.

I first read Doubinsky's *Song of Synth* (Black Coffee Press, 2013) and thought it was already being hailed as a masterpiece. To my disbelief my assumptions were wrong. The book had its fans, its place in the community, sure, but nothing like the fanfare I anticipated. In retrospect, now I know the man behind the novel, I wonder how much of this was down to Seb's own reluctance to transcend his role as indie darling and achieve the heights of SF stardom. Who's to say—but I have now read every book Doubinsky has written (every book in English anyway) and each one steams with the trademark of a ubiquitous talent. That's not just me blowing smoke either.

I remember sending Seb a letter of appreciation, fan mail basically, telling him how wonderful I thought *Song of Synth* was. I had a book out myself, but, frankly, it was bloody terrible, and I felt sure a writer of Doubinsky's calibre would ignore any attempts at Facebook correspondence from a complete nobody—in my head the Vandyke facial hair and stern-faced B&W author photo suggested all the trappings of a crapulous, irritable artiste. To my astonishment, he replied. Her replied *thanking* me and proceeded to send me the hardback double novel edition of *Synth/Absinth* from PS Publishing. From that day Seb has been my main mentor. I'm marginally more than a complete nobody today because of him and his guidance.

I found other writers out there, some established, some novice, who held Seb is similar high regard. I had an idea to compile an anthology of writers who were inspired by his style and his character. Other people who wanted to say thank you to someone who always puts others before himself, sometimes to his own detriment.

You should know, Seb is an everyman. A wonderful writer. A remarkable friend and teacher. But what makes him truly unique, though, is that he's oblivious to all these things. I suppose this is just another fan-letter. At least this time he's powerless but to sit back and take the bloody compliment...

Hope, the Killer

Ted Fauster

The rapidly darkening sky cast a pall over the southern canal district of Sorgbjerg, threatening dirty snow but for the moment producing only a sterile and windless cold.

Beneath it all, Luuk Maru pulled the long rubber coat tight and tucked the cardboard box beneath one arm. Hurrying from the sterility of the practically empty train, he emerged onto the tilted sidewalk that skirted the now deserted Potemkin Perimeter Station with a deep and irrepressible scowl carved onto his face.

"Shit," he said to the sky as the train hissed then slowly pulled away. It quickly sped and in seconds was swallowed by the dark until only a fading ball of yellow vapor remained.

The train had been inexcusably delayed and it was now far later in the day than Luuk had anticipated. Flicka would be asleep. He'd missed her birthday. He would have to wait until morning to give her the doll. He clenched his teeth as he tromped along.

"Buncha fuckin' shit."

In this no-man's-land between districts, the federal dividing line consisted of a broad canal contained by a tall, electrified chain-link fence, capped with unforgiving shark-tooth wire. The barrier rose in stark contrast to the artificial city park that sloped down from the jowls of the city to the north to merge with the pockmarked concrete that cupped the canal.

Two worlds forced to face one another. Separate yet conjoined. Sickly symbiotic. Beyond the city lay the Industrial District where men like Luuk built things that people who lived in the city used.

Like most no-creds, Luuk lived in a small, hovel of an apartment on the other side of the fence, in the less than desirable neighborhood of Alouise, a place where there were no coffee shops or cafés, no art galleries or museums, no real sense of community or safety.

The day was gone. A Tuesday. A waste, really. His first of only four days off had evaporated.

For Luuk, it had been a long, shitty work cycle and he was tired. He wanted nothing more than to get to the spot where the flit he'd ordered from the train would pick him up and take him home to his family, his wife and two children. This cycle had lasted nearly six weeks. Six long weeks. It was time to go home.

Up ahead in the dark he spied the vague suggestion of the gray-green dome of the rotunda. He sniffed and grabbed the box tighter. *Almost there.*

The buttery glow of a lamppost drew his eye, and within the cone of light he spotted a familiar cluster of prostitutes pressed shoulder to shoulder on one of the heated plastic park benches. He kept moving, hunching forward and lowering his eyes to avoid their calculating stares. To his relief, they taunted only halfheartedly as he passed, shivering in solidarity, thumbing their noses at his silence as he shuffled his boots in practiced patterns to keep from losing his footing in the slush.

Synth intensified the already bold reds and yellows of a neon hoverpanel adverting some trendy new clothing line. It filled the trees with colored lanterns and the hookers with helium. A few of the girls bloated and wiggled loose to float high up into the star-flecked sky where they shrunk to tiny dots.

Luuk squeezed his eyes shut and kept walking. The drug meant no harm. He knew that. On some level he was actually comforted by its tenacity. But the work cycle was over. Like his containment suit, the habit had to be carefully folded and tucked away, hermetically sealed and stored until the next work cycle began.

The Industrial District was miles away. After boarding the train he'd passed straight through the heart of the city like a dart. Nonstop. The federal train would never stop to allow him or anyone like him off. He was what he was and it was good enough.

Luuk never looked out the window. Arms folded across his chest, he always kept his head down and dozed, allowing his body to be gently rocked back and forth to the listing rhythm of the train like an empty shell at the bottom of the sea. In his mind, the times he would spend away from the foundry, however brief, often bloomed.

From his pocket he pulled his federal phone, slid a thumb across the glass. A green dot blipped on a digital map. The flit would arrive soon. He stood in the cold by the curb, waiting.

As a no-cred, it had taken nearly two decades to rehab his financial status to a point where he could make subtle purchases. Rent work clothes. Pay for testing. Secure an apartment. A home of his own would forever remain an impossibility. That was a demon he'd faced long ago. But at least now his family was safe. Off the streets. At least he had accomplished that.

When the foundry job became available he did not hesitate. Jobs there were very hard to come by. You simply did not pass them up. He would stay as long as the company could make use of him, as long as his tired body could hold up. What came after that was something he simply never considered.

In the fog of his own thoughts he'd left a fresh pack of Navis on the train. A cigarette would have been good, especially in the cold. There was a pack at home, in the medicine cabinet. He licked his lips in anticipation and plunged both hands deep into the pockets of the coat.

In the pocket to which he'd returned the phone, his fingers found and then began to roll a reassuring clot of tiny black pellets between forefinger and thumb through the worn skin of a plastik bag.

Old friend. Old ally. Sleep. Sleep for now.

From out of the gloom two globes of light appeared. With a droning mechanical whir, the flit pulled close to the curb and Luuk hurried to lift the door just as the blackness above released a pelting of rain. He sniffed as he slid across the bench.

"Alouise Station," he said with as little personality as possible. "West side."

The driver turned, laying a big hairy arm across the top of the front bench seat. Luuk's wristband clicked. The lingering influence of Synth made the man's eyes roil like storm clouds and the thick whiskers on his chiseled face wriggle like eels.

"Lucky you," the driver said, raising two caterpillar brows. He turned, shifted his weight, and the flit raced off.

This vehicle was newer, Luuk noticed. Not the usual musty car most drivers used. Smelled almost clean. The backseat was comfortable and there was a ventilated pane of plastik separating the front of the vehicle from the rear, not just a mesh of wire.

"Yeah," Luuk managed with a cough, not really caring what the man had meant by that. "Hey, you wouldn't have a cigarette, would you?"

"Nah, I use a snifter now. Much cleaner. Hits you fast." The flit slowed and waited for an opening into a driving circle. When one appeared the driver gunned the vehicle and they shot out into a swirling soup of cars.

Luuk righted himself. Brushed back a lock of mousy brown hair. "Yeah, but nothing beats a goddamn cigarette," he muttered.

Two blue marbles appeared in the rearview. "How 'bout cancer? That trump a tobacco stick?" Outside a horn blared. Dopplered as it swiftly passed. "Costs a lot to get rid of cancer. You know, my father wouldn't quit either. Kept smoking until—"

"I like to smoke," Luuk said with finality.

An uncomfortable silence descended and remained the entire way over the bridge and down into Alouise Station, the west side. Luuk called up the last of the drug but it had already faded.

At the stop he exited without thanking the man and the flit sped away, leaving him standing at the foot of a crooked tower of concrete and iron that rose before him in a bluish smear against the blackened sky. No stars here.

In the dripping remnants of the rain shower Luuk gazed up at the old building. So massive. Solid. Real. Whoever had built it had meant it for some other purpose but that didn't mean shit now. This towering stone edifice was his home. At least one tiny cube within it. And it wasn't going anywhere.

Somewhere, off in the distance, a dog barked then began to howl. With a sigh only he could understand, Luuk slowly crossed the filthy asphalt.

After just a few paces he froze and his chest tightened. He

patted his coat. The box. The box with the doll. He'd left it in the flit.

In a state of mild panic, he pulled out his phone. Clicked on the app. Fired off a quick message. A canned response appeared, something about how the driver was busy but would return his message soon. In the cold, in the gloom, in the limp spritzing piss of rain, Luuk waited nearly half an hour before going inside.

"Soup's on the stove," Sempki called from the kitchen the moment the front door snapped shut. As he drew off his coat and shook it dry Luuk took a big sniff. Lentil. With basil. What was she still doing up?

"Be right there," he defeatedly called back as he pulled off his boots and set them by the fire to dry, knowing full well his wife's voice had already reverberated up into the loft. Moments later a flurry of footfalls sounded on the wooden steps and Luuk turned to watch as two beaming children dressed in nightshirts appear at the foot of the stairs. Besso was still wiping the sleep from his eyes. His golden-haired sister stepped in front of him and stood grinning from ear to ear.

"Hello Papa," Flicka said exuberantly. She stood at attention with her hands at the small of her back. Eyes beaming expectantly. "It's my birthday today. Did you know that?"

Luuk nearly teared. "Yes, my lovely."

"I'm..." she counted in her head. Held up a bundle of fingers. "...*four* today!"

"You're three," Sempki corrected. Luuk shot her a look and the tired woman shrugged. She'd been beautiful once. Or perhaps he had imagined that. Now his wife only looked tired and dirty all the time. She caught him staring, balled up a fist on her hip and gave a curt nod.

"Well then? The present?"

Luuk turned back to the girl. "Yes... well..." His mind raced like a pinwheel in a hurricane. He held up a finger. "That's coming right up, my lovely. But first papa must step out for a moment to purchase some cigarettes. You understand."

Flicka scrunched up her face. "Oh papa, cigarettes make your breath smell awful."

"There's a pack in the medicine cabinet," Sempki insisted, and Luuk frowned at her.

"Stale," he fired back.

As quickly as he could, Luuk pulled his coat back on. Besso had wandered back upstairs the moment he realized there was no present to examine. Flicka hopped up and down.

"No, papa, no! You don't need them. Instructor says..."

But Luuk was already at the fire, pulling on his boots. He rushed to the door. It unsnapped and he stepped out into the hall, pushing it shut behind him.

Out on the streets the rain had started again, but it was only a soft drizzle. Luuk walked briskly over the humped and broken sidewalk, hoping against hope that the newsstand was still open, as it sometimes was.

From deep in his chest came a thump and he pulled the neck of the coat tight. Acid from his stomach. Up into his throat. Burning like kerosene.

Luuk clenched his teeth. Walked faster. He could see the lights of the newsstand now. Beneath the radiance some kids loitered, ringlets of snifter gas rising up from their huddled faces.

Luuk still hadn't learned the name of the man who ran the stand, but he was always there when it was open. Passing through the kids, he pointed and the man turned to retrieve one of the red-and-yellow packs. Was it too late? How do you ask the name of someone you've seen a half dozen times?

"Forty-three kroners," the man said, slapping the pack down onto the wooden counter. He kept his fat fingers on top of the pack. In his other hand was a scan gun.

Luuk smiled at the man as he peeled back the cuff of his coat. He stuck out the wristband. "Nice of the rain to let up," he said. The man shrugged as he scanned. Luuk cleared his throat. Beside him the boys giggled and bounced.

"I don't mind the rain," the man said as he pressed buttons on the gun. "Clears the shit from the sky." He looked up. "Anything else? Some whiskey? Rev?"

Rev was the federally approved, street-legal version of Synth. It was crap.

"No thanks." Luuk pocketed the pack. Squinted toward the back of the stall. He pointed. "How much for that?"

The man turned. "What? The roses? They're not real."

Luuk shook his head.

"No, the horse."

The man looked up at the crowded expanse of useless shit he had for sale, almost as if it had become nothing more than wallpaper long ago and he'd forgotten what was actually there. "I believe that's a seahorse," he said.

"Even better. How about the blue one."

The man reached up. Plucked a dusty package from one of the hooks. He studied it. Gave a sigh as he reached for the gun. Scanned it. The gun wouldn't read. He grumbled and wiped at the strip on the packaging. Scanned it again. A soft bleep.

"Fifteen kroners."

Luuk stuck out his wrist.

On the way back to the apartment, he passed an alley. Before he could get beyond its mouth, a raspy voice called out and he jumped.

"Easy," an older woman said from the gloom. She stepped into the sodium glow of a streetlamp and Luuk saw that she wore a sparkling green dress. She was rail thin. Amateurish makeup attempt. Teetering. "I won't bite."

Luuk waved her off. Made a move to keep walking. But she slinked in front of him with surprising speed and agility.

"Hey now," she said hoarsely. An unlit cigarette hung from her lower lip, somehow stuck there. Her eyes gave only a faint indication of awareness. "What's the rush?"

"Please," Luuk attempted. "It's my daughter's birthday."

"Yeah? What'dya get her?"

Luuk hesitated. He held up the seahorse package. The woman made a grab. This time he easily stepped around her and kept walking, ignoring the hail of insults that followed. One, however, struck oddly home.

"Too bad she won't be there when you're gone."

It could have meant anything. It could have meant nothing. He didn't even know why it had caused him to prickle. Some old hooker. Worn out street meat, that's all she was. He quickened his pace.

From his pocket he retrieved the pack of Navis. Peeled back the cellophane with his teeth. Spat out a thin rectangle of plastik. He jiggled out one long yellow stick and clamped it between his lips. Fumbled for the lighter and lit up.

Luuk inhaled deeply as he walked, pulling a nicotine ribbon deep into his lungs, until he could almost feel it touch his belly. He exhaled blissfully, feeling suddenly more alive, and watched as the smoke billowed up and expanded into the now clear night sky like an exorcised spirit. He was better now. More complete. But he realized his hands were still shaking.

Reflexively, one hand dropped to the coat pocket. Slipped inside to palm the plastik bag. Fiddled.

Luuk's eyes darted as he walked. Just one pellet. That should be enough. With a flick of his fingers he shot it into the back of his throat.

The pellet stuck and he swallowed hard. It dislodged and slipped down. A tiny time bomb in his gut. He sucked on the cigarette as he walked, hot-boxing it down like a fuse, greedily inhaling, pulling more poison down, down.

It didn't take long. By the time he reached the door to the apartment the strings had started.

Luuk held the handle so the door closed quietly behind him. When he turned the music rose subtly, soothing. The apartment felt warmer than it should have been. The rich aroma of lentil soup still hung in the air although the table was bare. The children were nowhere to be seen.

Luuk stepped lightly across a swirling mass of colors, a rich pageantry of rusty oranges, golds, and crawling moss and lichen. Beneath the sewing table he spied a rabbit casually chewing at the carpet. It watched him as he slowly drifted across the room as if on rails. The caramel door to the kitchen swung inward at his prompt.

Sempki was at the sink. Glitter in the air. Birds chirping. The clattering of the dishes added to the arrangement. Woodwinds. Brass. A crash of cymbals.

A swirl of brown draped seductively down in a long "s" into the curve of his wife's back where it seemed to indicate the way. The swaying curves of her hips beckoned, and like a leaf in a gurgling stream he became caught up within the orchestral orgasma. He came up behind her. Gently took hold of her waist, squeezed, and drew her rubbery flesh against the sturdy warmth of his pelvis.

Sempki whirled around and slapped him. "Can't you see I am trying to clean the mess you left behind?"

The strings scraped then stalled.

"The mess *I* left behind?"

She let the pot she was holding drop down into the bottom of the enamel sink. It clattered deafeningly. She flicked her wrist at it. "Each meal is a gift, Luuk. You know this. And what, what is this nonsense?"

Luuk found he was still holding onto the seahorse. He held it up. "There was a doll."

"Oh yes, a doll."

"Yes. I left it in the flit." Just then he thought of his phone. The message he'd sent. He fished it out, but Sempki was already undoing her apron. With a scowl, she tossed it aside and left the room, muttering.

At the stairs the children were back, Flicka clutching her tiny yellow blanket to her chest, looking up at him with sad eyes as her mother tromped by and hooked her arm. Luuk held out the seahorse and for a moment her eyes were drawn to it, but they widened and turned as Sempki drew her up the stairs. Her sleepy brother followed.

Luuk stood in the main room of the apartment. Alone. From the loft above he heard the lamp click, and the apartment went dim, only the light from the muted wallscreen dancing on the faded plaster walls. He turned to face it.

A grainy protest spread across the screen. Pixelated and distorted. Likely shot from an older model phone in shaking hands. It looked like the person was running. In the frame, kids with paper signs darted about, shouting, throwing things. Fire in the background. Smoke. Men in brown body armor rushed in with batons and nets.

Luuk found the couch and dropped into it. With the seahorse in his hands, he lay back and shut his eyes. Behind his eyelids, Synth rattled like an angry tea kettle.

He woke to warm sunlight on his face. Despite this, it felt decidedly cool. Conditioned. Luuk rustled. From somewhere close he could sense the sea, could actually smell the sunlight in the air. He opened his eyes.

The room was a blush of white and seafoam. Somehow comforting in its sterility. On the sheets beside him was his wife, still sleeping. She had her pale back to him and long red ribbons of hair lay scattered against a sea of crisp white. Through the bright rectangle over her shoulder Luuk's eyes warmed to a steady canvas of blue framed by two thin curtains of more white. Lena stirred and rolled toward him. Her lids lifted and her freckled face spread into a warm smile.

"Morning," she breathed.

Small, tender hands scuttled beneath the sheets. They found his bare chest and continued, spiderlike, until they were up at his neck. Beneath the sheets she was naked, a speckled slip of alabaster and pink. She moaned as he rolled into her.

Afterward, out on the porch, espressos in hand, they stared down at the surf. White, lazy ribbons curling over pearl blue. From the infinitely clear sky above gulls cried, and down on the immaculate white sand more pecked at the retreating rivulets. Lena looked over from her chair and Luuk smiled at her.

"Did you have the dream again?"

Luuk gave a low chuckle, lifted his tiny porcelain cup and sipped. "How did you know?"

"You were a little clammy. You're never clammy."

Luuk stared out across the ocean. Everything looked so big. Wild and endless.

"It's just a dream."

"It's not just a dream." Her voice had changed. Taken on the lawyer tone. "Remember what Dr. Nelson said. It's from the Synth."

Luuk huffed. "It's not the Synth."

This was an ongoing battle, but one he always won. Synth was safe. Synth worked. As a visual artist it helped expand his mind more than any drug he'd ever tried, and he was always able to keep his head. When he was done being creative, a shot of medmezine bleached it out of his system and he was back to his old self.

"It's like I told you," he explained for the umpteenth time. "It's a switch. A creative switch. I can turn it on and off as I please. I'm in total control."

Lena sighed. She always sighed. More than anyone she knew Synth kept them in luxury. Very few of Viborg City's citizens had even seen the coast of Kong Christian, let alone been given a license to own a home there. They were part of a lucky few, the elite, and they owed a good portion of it to the illegal version of a watered-down recreational drug most could never dream of affording.

They had it all. The houses. The cars. The memberships, yachts, and political influence. Rarely had an artist risen to such high standings. It was practically unheard of.

"I was thinking we could go down to the market today. I'd like to get some fresh flowers for tonight's party and—"

"Tonight's party?"

Lena smiled patiently. "Yes, Luuk." Behind her a smattering of puffy white clouds appeared in the sky. "Don't you remember?"

Then he suddenly did. Victor and Helena were coming over. And Marcus and Adele. He nodded.

"Yes, oh yes. Very sorry. I'd forgotten."

"Yes, well, the other day I saw they had sunflowers, and poppies and dahlias. Wouldn't that look nice?" He supposed it would and said so. "I thought we could get washed up and go down for some lunch out on the wharf, and then wander through the district for—"

"I have some work to finish," he cut in as politely as he could. "Very sorry. I'm at a critical juncture. You understand." He smiled diplomatically.

Lena's smile dimmed and was immediately replaced by a mildly confused expression.

"Um... of course, my love." She gave a nod and the smile puffed back into existence. "I understand."

"But you go," he added as she rose from the chair. With a twist of his wrist he downed the last of the espresso. "I'm going to the studio and I won't be out until this afternoon. That okay?"

Of course it was. He'd only asked as a courtesy. Lena was, after all, his wife.

She paused to look back. Widened her smile. "Of course, my love. I can go on my own. Just please be dressed and ready by four."

Four it was. Plenty of time. The entire day to indulge.

Down in the studio he stood at one end of the room, staring at the broken column. Fixed to the top was a small dollhouse painted gray, the front door glued shut, all of the windows blacked out. All but one. On a long wire strung down from the high ceiling hung a single speaker.

Through it, the recording of the old Portuguese woman reciting the Lord's Prayer played over and over in a loop. The recording had been collected on an old telephone with very poor reception. It crackled and popped as the old woman droned on and on.

The installation was nearly complete. Technically speaking. The column, the dollhouse, the speaker and recording. Those were all solidly in place. It was the insides of the house that concerned Luuk.

Standing with his chin in one hand, the other hand supporting his elbow, Luuk stared around the studio and waited for the drugs to kick in.

The interior of the dollhouse was key, the anchor to the entire installation. Viewers were encouraged to approach, to look inside the one unclouded window. But what would they see?

Synth took over, wrapped the old woman's voice in color. Blues and greens reached down from the speaker like rainforest vines to ensnare the toy home. That was another secret. Around the back of the display was a cellar door that suggested a basement. The door lifted to reveal a tiny cubby lined with blue velvet. Inside would be a cache of black pellets, military-grade Synth.

Synth would transform the installation into a unique masterpiece for whomever was wise enough to explore and indulge. He'd leave clues, of course. Somehow. Somehow, with whatever it was viewers would witness taking place inside.

Luuk stared. For nearly an hour he continued to stare. Nothing was coming. He'd been at this too long, had stared at his own work for countless hours. It was like sampling scented candles in a shop and going smell-blind. They used beans to cure that. Coffee beans. Luuk needed some beans of his own.

He turned his back on the display. Walked straight to the wall and hit the switch that turned the recording off. The room fell immediately silent. Below the switch was a glass cart filled with bottles.

Whiskey. Vodka. Tequila...

Luuk's eyes widened.

Absinthe.

It was wormwood. Nothing more. And synthesized wormwood at that. For real wormwood to provide any hallucinogenic effects it would have to be present in amounts that could easily cause permanent brain damage, even death.

Luuk lifted the slender green bottle. Held it up to the light that shone in from the room's lone window. The dragon on the label noticed him and writhed in response. This shit had been expensive. It worked without the Synth. What it could accomplish when combined was anyone's guess.

Luuk checked his wristwatch. Eleven. Plenty of time.

He made sure to use the bathroom. To smoke one last cigarette out on the sun deck. He didn't want the installation to smell like smoke, although it likely wouldn't matter.

Luuk woke to the sound of the commuter train rambling past the building. His eyes opened. Still dark. Still cold. The fire must have gone out. And in a rush he remembered.

This isn't real, he suddenly knew. *This isn't... me!*

He sat up in the bed and Sempki gave a soft moan. Across the foot of the bed lay Flicka, having gotten up from the pile of blankets some time during the night. Or perhaps her brother had hogged the warmest ones. Indeed, he was still there on the floor, blissfully ignorant of any wrongdoing.

Despite the cold, Luuk broke out into a sweat. He felt different. Older. Fatter. Less healthy. Taking care not to wake anyone, he crept from the creaking bed and slipped downstairs.

At the bottom of the apartment the cold ran through his bones like an electrical charge, waking him. He recalled his initial thoughts when he had woken. Silly. He shook his head. Of course this was real.

His coat was hanging by the door. In one pocket he found the pack of Navis. Pulled one out. Lit it and inhaled. The smoke in his lungs reassured him. He'd had a dream. Only a dream. Albeit a kind of pleasant one, it had only existed for the briefest of moments in his head.

Still, the smell of the ocean, the feel of his...

He thought of Sempki and felt immediately guilty. She was his wife. And she had given them two beautiful children. He sniffed in the dark. Found a lantern. Lit it. The apartment glowed to life. He went to the smoldering fire and rekindled it with more peat, making sure it was blazing hot before climbing the stairs and crawling back into bed. None of his family was any the wiser.

Morning came with the barking of dogs. A built-in and dependable alarm in Alouise District. Out in the hall the stairs soon boomed with footfalls and voices. Men and women shuffling off to work. Children's voices too, the ones whose parents could afford to send them to school. Luuk's children learned from home. When they could. They were still young. There would be time enough to prepare them for the workforce. For now, he and Sempki were perfectly content to have them around and keep them fed in a building that did not leak or let in too much of the cold.

While Sempki cooked, the children played at Luuk's feet. Besso with his ball and jacks, and Flicka with the seahorse. Her brother had shown only mild interest when she'd opened it and had left her alone, although he now seemed to have reconsidered and was in the early stages of some dedicated lobbying to enlist his sister in the undersea exploration of a labyrinthine network of caves he'd constructed of chair legs and bunched up portions of carpet. Flicka was presently unimpressed and would likely require much more convincing.

Luuk looked down from his cup of coffee with a labored smile. This was his life. *This* was his life.

He took another sip. Sempki was calling. He thought of Lena.

Such pale skin. So immaculately smooth...

When his wife called louder he shook out of his reverie and gathered up the children to join Sempki in the kitchen.

"May we eat upstairs?" Besso asked, his usual morning request. And as usual, Sempki shook her head without so much as looking at him.

"You may not. When I was a little girl we all gathered every morning to eat around the kitchen table," she said as she ladled porridge into stone bowls. "We're lucky to have enough room in our kitchen to have a table. Did you know that?"

"Yes, mama," the children said in unison. Sempki smiled at her work, then over at Luuk. And Luuk felt the shame all over again.

"Yes," he said. "We're very lucky, indeed."

The day was no time for lounging. Shortly after breakfast, Luuk left his wife and children and went down to the docks, to the job he occasionally took as a lift operator. He didn't mind it so much. Lift operators were paid fairly well and the job was not nearly as physically taxing as his job at the foundry, although it was dreadfully monotonous.

No Synth here. Synth evaporated quickly from the bloodstream, allowing users to show up safely for most non-federal jobs. Drugs were not allowed outside of the city, and never for non-federal workers. Of course, many did partake. And many found themselves very rapidly unemployed. Luuk was no fool. He could take the occasional six hours on his backside with ease. They could always use the money. There was never enough.

When the day was over and he was walking back home

through the alleyways he thought of the dream again. He'd had it before. Or at least suspected he had. But why was it sticking so much this time?

Was it the sex? Surely it could have been. To his amazement, he was able to recall every aspect of the interlude. Surely it had been a dream. Surely it had.

Perhaps it was the Synth. Perhaps he had reached some kind of threshold, some point in his habit where his mind had simply fractured open and spilled into some other consciousness. He'd heard of hardcore users losing their grasp on reality, of believing the most berserk things. But those were the deviants, the ones who mixed other far more dangerous drugs with Synth. From what he knew, Synth had been manufactured by the military as a social coping mechanism, a means for soldiers to maintain their sanity when deployed to hazardous areas. Used properly, Synth could even heal. At least that's what he'd heard.

Of course, no one Luuk knew used the drug for those sorts of purposes. While the hallucinogenic properties did take some getting used to, it was no different than a harmless daydream. It simply took time to recognize the enhancements to your surroundings and to separate what was real from what was synthesized. In proper doses, Synth made an otherwise miserable work experience actually somewhat bearable.

That evening, Luuk decided to perform an experiment, without informing his wife, of course. Sempki knew full well he used the drug. She even knew he occasionally imbibed at home. They'd spoken about it. Her only insistence was that he not use it around the children. He'd broken that rule the other night, but that was only out of an immediate need. The old woman in the alley had caught him off guard, and he'd just come off an unusually long shift, had just lost his daughter's birthday gift.

Before crawling back into bed, Luuk popped a single pellet then quickly drifted off to sleep.

Luuk woke to Lena's shaking.

"Darling," she said loudly as she shook him by the shoulders. "Darling, you have to wake up. You have to get ready. Our guests will be here soon."

Luuk picked himself up from the floor, stood and looked around. He was still in the studio. He hadn't done a thing new on the installation.

"I'm... I'm so sorry," he said. "I must have fallen asleep."

Lena helped him to the elevator and into the bedroom where she sat him in a chair by a window overlooking the shoreline. Already the sun was dropping and the waves were growing bolder. From the bathroom he heard the shower turn on.

"Please hurry," Lena called to him. "We haven't much time. Our guests will be here soon and I still need you to go down into the cellar and select the wine." She was in the room now, lifting him, helping him remove his smock and t-shirt. "Do you need me to go over the menu with you?"

Luuk shook his head. "No, my love. That's not necessary."

He remembered the menu, already knew what he would select. The '65 Cab Franc for the amuse bouche, the chilled Soave for the soup, a good Beaujolais for the appetizers and salad, and a full-bodied Syrah for the veal. He pondered the desert wine in the shower, not quite having figured that one out just yet. But Lena was making her soufflé, and you simply couldn't go wrong with a good Port.

Four o'clock saw the first pair arrive, Victor and Helena. Victor was a balding market analyst and Helena was a plump brunette loudmouth who did something or other in finance. Together they were delightful. Separate them and they were a bore and a bleeding earful, in that order.

The two couples wasted no time in waiting for Marcus and Adele, who would arrive late, as always, and simply relaxed with Martinis on the upper balcony until the latecomers were announced.

Marcus, a short man in spectacles, ran a small investment firm and despised vodka, so no harm no foul. Ridiculously slender and buxom, Adele towered over him, and frequently pushed him away whenever he drew near, which he did quite frequently at even the tiniest of get-togethers. They blended right in with the others, who by now had had their fill of vodka and were ready for dinner.

The meal went without a hitch, seeming to Luuk like so many other dinner-parties he and Lena had carefully organized. The food varied but the conversation usually did not. Once again there was politics and religion, the homeless and the wars.

On this particular evening, Luuk felt a bit stranger than usual. It had to have been the absinthe. His system was quite used to Synth, and it had been hours since he had dropped a pellet anyway. Still, he felt altogether odd and was having difficulty focusing on the conversation. The two cocktails likely did not help, nor did the wine with his food.

"Did you hear what I was saying?" Helena directed at him from across the table. Luuk was not entirely surprised to see coils of golden snakes in her hair.

"Uh... no, Helena. I'm very sorry. I did not."

Lena gave an awkward laugh. "He's been so busy on his latest installation," she said in his defense. "It's been a rather difficult one to complete."

"Well, that's not entirely true," Luuk interjected. "It's just been something of a... of a challenge, I suppose."

"Well then," Victor said as he chewed, "tell us all about it."

His eyes, Luuk noticed, were bulging nearly out of his head and his fork and knife were rubber.

"Uh... I..."

"It's something with the Lord's Prayer, isn't it, dear?"

Luuk felt sweat beading on his forehead. He lifted his napkin. Quickly dabbed. "Well, yes. I suppose you could say—"

"Religion is always a hot button," Helena tossed in. "Isn't that true?"

"Well of course it is," Marcus added. "I mean, all you have to do is mention any particular savior figure and you'll have a good portion of the room up in arms." He chuckled.

"Oh, I agree," Adele said. "There are far too many religions these days. And far too many people becoming offended."

Luuk could only stare at her chest. A crew of cockroaches

had just finished using steak knives to cut her breasts free from her gown, allowing each of them to lift off and float across the room like pink zeppelins.

Luuk dropped the napkin and coughed. He flushed.

"Darling," Lena said to him. "Are you all right?"

Luuk stood and pushed out his chair. "I'm very sorry," he said to the room. "I'm not feeling well. I... I believe I'll get some air."

Luuk raced to the nearest set of doors, out onto the back patio and down a long flight of concrete stairs until he was on the beach. There he ran across the sand, all the way to the shore, certain he was going to vomit. He did so in the surf, then stood with his hands on his knees, still woozy, the surf rolling up to his shoes. Lena caught up with him and draped an arm across his shoulder.

"Darling, what is it? Should I call an ambulance?"

Luuk shook his head. He could hear the noise of the surf growing louder and louder, drowning out the sound of his wife's voice.

Then he saw it. At his feet in the surf. A tiny brown seahorse. When he bent to lift it from the sand his ears popped.

"Oh my," his wife whispered at his side. "I hear they've been showing up all over the shore. Something to do with the warming seas, or maybe pollution or something."

Luuk could only stare down at the tiny creature in his palm. It felt brittle against his skin, wooden. But when its tail suddenly uncurled he knew it was real. He bent to place it back into the water and the surf swept in and took it. Over the pounding of the tide he heard something else, a voice that called more insistently.

"Luuk!"

Luuk sat up in bed. He was freezing.

Sempki draped a blanket around him, pulled him close.

"My God, you're bathed in sweat and shivering," she said, but he pulled away. In the gloom, his wife sat curiously staring at him.

"What?" she asked "What is it?"

Slowly, Luuk shook his head. "I know now," he said.

His wife remained confused. "Know what?"

"I know what to put inside the dollhouse."

Sempki stared at him for a very long time. Then she rolled over and said. "Mind the fire, will you? It's still so damn cold."

There were a few things he needed. Once he was certain Sempki was back asleep, Luuk crept out of bed and carefully made his way downstairs. On the way he stepped barefoot on the plastic seahorse, but he didn't stop.

From his coat near the door he pulled out the plastik bag of pellets, tore it open and swallowed them all. There was a beer in the kitchen. Half of one on the counter. With what remained he hydrated the pellets in his stomach. When he found what he was looking for, he rushed back up to the loft where he discovered Flicka sitting upright on the floor.

"Papa, what is it?"

Luuk held a finger to his nose. He sat down next to the girl and put an arm around her. With his other arm he reached around to grab hold of the leading edge of the roll of plastik wrap he'd retrieved from the kitchen and stretched it across her face.

To his surprise, the girl did not scream. She hardly even struggled. Maybe she wasn't supposed to. He pulled out more plastik, kept wrapping it around her head until her skin blued and her eyes bulged and she went limp. When he laid her gently down against the blankets Besso sat staring at him in confusion.

"Papa, what are you doing?"

"Shh," Luuk said to the boy, drawing him near. He hugged him close and tight, so tight he could hear the vertebrae in his spine pop. When the boy moaned and tried to push away the tears came, but Luuk held on. He knew better now. This was the only way.

Luuk squeezed tighter and tighter, slipping a hand up to take the boy by the neck. But before he could give it a twist, the fire iron slammed into his forehead.

Luuk saw white, and he fell back against the floorboards.

Something warm and wet drooled down his forehead and over his face. His ears rang but he could hear the boy crying now, could make out the sounds of his wife screaming, saw her face twisted above him in rage.

"I am a man of dignity," he said up to her. "A man of great means. I don't belong here."

Sempki glared down at him as if he were a demon. She lifted the iron and he held up a hand, but it wasn't to block the blow.

"It's okay," he managed to say. "You won't remember any of this."

The blow was fierce. Vengeful. It had surely split the flesh of his skull wide open. Sempki heaved and another blow descended, severing his vision. Intense pain, like a bursting sun. Then another blow and another.

The world dimmed. Some other broken world. It didn't matter. Only a trap. Nothing here mattered. It could happen this way or the other. The prison walls would soon burst and the truth would break free.

Haiku Hidden Within the Song of Synth

Ole Hardcore

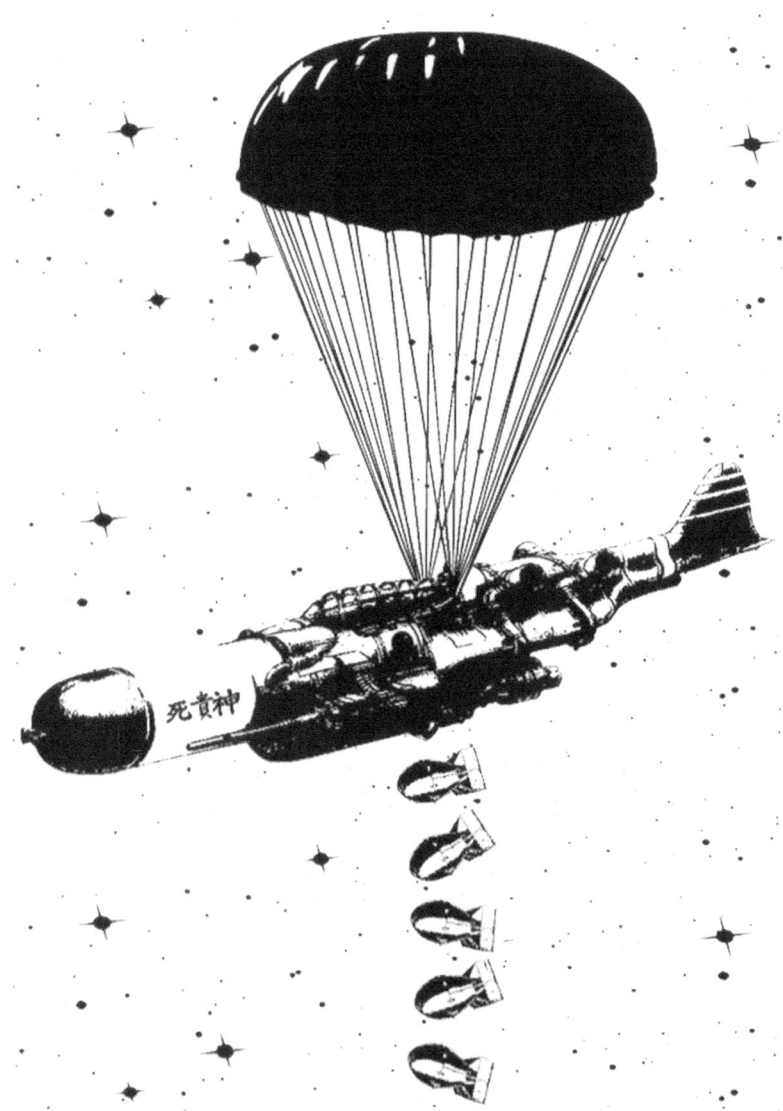

Sehnsucht

Old melancholy
Centuries of poets
past illusions

Orb

A golden cradle
distant flute melody
Hearts refuge

Earth-shaped

Bathroom door
Fragmented beauty splinters
Karen screaming

Bus

Towards nothingness
An uncertain death
end of all routes

Ole

Synths silhouette
red tie behind a bar
eternal beer

Wind

Urchin kicks the ball
the card in the garbage
run little bandit

The Life of Bodhi
(Quelling a Worker's Strike)

Jonathan Moon

(for Seb)

Bodhi was born in a tent on the outskirts of New Babylon. His clan sang songs, rattled bows of alder wood lined with bells, beat drums with their hands, and danced around the tent- their celebration drowning out his screeching entrance into the world. Strings of bright lights lined the interior of the tent, bundles of sage and rapeseed burned in battered ceremonial trays of tin and bronze, his first moments were a whirlwind of overwhelming sensations. He was held into the air and his clan approached, one by one, pressing their thumbs to the middle of his tiny forehead, and they each whispered to him ancient traditional blessings and personal welcomes.

Before he was taking his first clumsy steps his family immigrated to Viborg City, drawn by the promises of opportunity, the advertised democracy and freedom, and all the glitz and glamor and convenience of success. Instead, they found the ghettos of Sorgbjerg; its narrow, filthy streets, its crowded, dilapidated tenements, and its overall despair ambiance. Gone were the vibrantly lit tent walls, breathing with the wind gusts, replaced with drab, nicotine yellowed walls. Gone was the cluster of tents, the clan crowded into studios and one-bedroom apartments, sleeping in rows across the floors and in the closets. Gone were the week-long celebrations of traditional holidays with extended clan and family, replaced with small, secretive celebrations held away from the judging eyes of Viborg City where nearly all aspects of their culture had been outlawed.

Bodhi knew his clan's name, was taught its rich and storied history in hushed tones at the kitchen table, yet nearly everybody in Viborg City called them 'Gypsies'. It mattered not what his clan was named, or what name the people across the hall

41

claimed- the thirteen of them squeezed so tightly into a single bedroom unit they would peel the tattered wall paper when they all moved at once. The elderly couple two doors down with their six grandchildren, came from two rival clans; at one time their union would have been seen as momentous and the six screaming grandchildren coloring the walls and linoleum floor and tipping house plants from their vases would have been seen as heirs to a new legacy of peace and tranquility. None of that mattered now, what names they called each other, themselves. In Viborg City they were all Gypsy.

Bodhi went to school when the city told him it was time. His clan elders argued with his parents to maintain the traditional ways of learning, to honor his traditional birth, the last of its kind for his clan. His father and mother resisted. The traditional ways held no sway, no benefit, no increased chance of success in Viborg City. The city would educate young Bodhi in ways which would best improve the chances of his success; his cultural ways would only get him outcast, punished, or worse. If he did well with the education the city provided perhaps his children would know the more comfortable life in of the Creds in the H.C. Andersen district. Perhaps they could live in a house, with a yard around it and rooms for each of them and windows with views of more than the closet crumbling building. With the education the city offered there was at least the 'perhaps' his parents argued the elders, and his cultural ways could not even offer that to the child.

The elders admitted their defeat in the face of his parents' defensiveness and determination. As they left the crowded kitchen they hung their gray heads, hunched their shoulders against the insult they felt. They mumbled their worries to each other, they worried the death of their storied history, they worried the empty bellies of the moment, and they worried the frightening omens of the future.

One, Poppa Rowden, saw young Bodhi peeking out from his hiding spot. He pointed at the boy with one long gnarled finger.

"Best to bleach his hair now, lighten his skin with the

same powder the prostitutes use. Better to rename him now, in celebration of his birth unto White City. Name him Hans, and hold steady against the waves of Cred as they roll in."

The old man's tone, much more so than his confusing words, frightened young Bodhi down to his quivering core. He stood from his place in the shadows and screamed at the menacing old man.

"No! I am Bodhi! And I am a Gypsy!"

Everyone cried then. The apartment wailed as one heaving emotional beast, a worm squirming against a lair it has outgrown. Little Bodhi had no idea what had caused them such anguish. He only knew no one looked to comfort him, and somehow he had disrespected his entire clan. He ran then. He ran and hid in the bathroom sink cabinet. He fell asleep hugging his knees curled against the cold plumbing, and woke up wondering if he would be Bodhi or Hans when his clan saw him again. He wondered who he really wanted to be.

It didn't matter. No one was talking. His parents were not talking to each other or the elders or him. And they didn't for what felt like a long while. The clan found itself swept up in the waves of humanity of Viborg City- the Red City, and when those waves broke against the red brick tenements of Sorgbjerg the clan was battered and fractured, twitching in the rumble and barley clinging to life. The wounds the immigration had split across them were deep, and they scarred over slowly- remaining raw enough they nearly always carried risk of being scraped away with any misspoken word or opinion. For much of his youth Bodhi was nearly as afraid to talk about what he learned at school as he was the traditional lessons stubborn aunts, uncles, poppas, and memaws whispered to him when he was out of his parents' earshot.

In time, the only identity which felt safe was the one which broke the clans' collective heart, the one which was thrust upon them all by the dominate culture, but the only one which captured the true spirit of the culture emerging as clans new and old, ally and rival, converged in Sorgbjerg. He was Bodhi, and he was a Gypsy. In time, they would all wear the name like their tattered wardrobes- with a fashionable mix of shame and pride.

They were Gypsies, and they occupied the bottom rung of a social ladder the city refused to acknowledge, much less address. Their labor kept the city glowing and clean and drawing in more citizens, it was they who sucked the shit from its septic tanks and cleared the filth from the streets, and they did it for wages that like the great city itself only offered a *chance* at survival. They were the most hated, and one of the most economically vital, social components of the Viborg City.

Bodhi learned all the city schools taught him. He learned to spell words, and place them in sentences, and to place those sentences together to form paragraphs, essays, and papers. He learned to add and subtract numbers, to multiply and divide and quantify and reduce and on and on. He learned history, biology, chemistry, ecology, economics and anything else they would teach him. But, Bodhi paid extra attention, and he learned lessons inside and outside of his classrooms. He learned about social structures and how they are built and how they are maintained. He learned about hate, and its many forms like the snarling heads of a hydra. He learned about chance, and luck, and how who he is, and the name he carried, would discount him of either. He learned about race and class and wealth. He learned about social machines, what greased their gears and who profited from their spewing toxic smokestacks. Before he left the city schools, Bodhi, Bodhi the Gypsy vowed to destroy that shambling, lying devil of a machine and to dance through the ashes of it with his people- the Gypsies- clans new and old, ally and rival, all converged upon Sorgbjerg.

Bodhi watched everyone around him as they fed themselves to the gears in order to keep the machine churning, to keep the lights glowing, to keep the mouths fed. He watched his mother and father, his aunts and uncles and cousins, limp home from 12 hour shifts- the burden of the clans' dreams crushing them all a little more with each passing day. The elders caught cancers from their factories and fields. The newborns showed the signs of heavy alcohol and synth use, most died in their cribs the first year. The clan was losing its past and its future, but Bodhi refused to allow it to fade away without a noble fight.

He watched his people starve while working themselves into early graves. He watched the city grow upon those graves, a macabre foundation of progress. He watched stress eat families up, rend them with teeth of sheer desperation, and shit them back out scattered amongst the other detritus littering the alleyways and streets of Sorgbjerg. He watched his classmates drop out of school; some to work minimum wage jobs, some to work street corners selling their innocence and orifices, and others to join up with criminal street gangs to make money through drugs and robbery. Bodhi saw all this and he knew he would need to do something different to survive, to ensure the survival of all his people, the survival of all the Gypsies.

Bodhi studied the people in the other two districts which made up Viborg City; the H.C. Andersen district where those who can afford Credit live and the luxurious Kong Kristian where the fortunate people who can exist on Cash live. He hypothesized the benefits to those other districts was a riddled equation, the solution to which could then be applied to the Gypsies of Sorgbjerg. He studied the geographic, economic, social, and political variances between the three districts and began his plotting.

Due to his academic perfection Bodhi earned diplomas, degrees, and, most importantly, job offers. Bodhi spent his meager life savings on three discount suits, hand-me-downs from Kong Kristian donation drives, and cultivated his image of confidence and success. He secured a job among the Creds in the Anderson district, working as an IT assistant for an idealistic far-left environmental monitoring company which claimed in their mission statement to be 'dedicated to clean air, land, and water for all citizens of Viborg City'. He was smart with his money, hoping an abundance of savings would be impressive when he earned the opportunity for Creds. However, when Bodhi received his 13th rejection notice on a Cred app it just happened to fall on the same fateful day when he discovered that his company suppressed their findings from a study into a bevy of chemicals Phoebus Cosmetics, the famous beauty products corporation, was pumping into the canals servicing greater Sorgbjerg. Bodhi walked out in mid-shift.

He saw the corruption infesting Viborg City, and how the racism and classism were the dead blackened veins under the city's pale porcelain skin. He pulled back; saw the famous Red City through a broader lens, and he saw the machine in its true form. He saw the gears, greased with the blood of his people, and he saw the cash spitting into the pockets of Kong Kristian corporate kingpins even as the sky above filled with noxious pillars of corpse-reeking smoke. Bodhi stared at the machine until his eyes burned, watered, and burned more. He examined every inch of it as it heaved and clattered and growled and glowed. He saw its iron-plating armor, the peoples' embedded ignorance and hate, buffed to a reflective sheen by the city's media streams, and he saw past all that armor to see the machine's fatal flaw.

Bodhi began organizing the Gypsy laborers, organizing not along occupations or professions, but along the imaginary borders between districts. He held candle-lit meetings in abandoned basements, opened and closed by traditional prayers, where he rallied people to his cause under a bandana mask to protect from the asbestos dust floating gently down from the ceiling above like so many shattered dreams. The meetings grew, desperate people drawn to his words of hope and action like moths to flames willing to flutter into the fire to keep themselves warm. The Gypsies had known their great crime of poverty and struggle all along, but Bodhi was teaching them weapons to fight those who defined the laws, those same people who forced the great crime to begin with.

His words spread, his ideas spread, and, inevitably his reputation spread outside of Sorgbjerg to the ears of those he was arming his people against. Bodhi saw the war brewing; saw his enemy- the machine- slowly becoming aware of the rising dissent when the gears began to grind within it as the workers began to deny it their blood to the inner workings which depended on running slick with it. The enemy generals wore suits which cost more than Bodhi's crumbling red brick tenement, and when they sent him a summons to discuss a peaceful, productive discourse to the budding labor strike he was organizing he burned his suits in a trashcans and wore his clan's traditional garb- so brilliantly colored against the gleaming White City office building where he would meet some of the city's most powerful employers and policy makers.

Bodhi, Bodhi the Gypsy, stood colorful, tall and proud before a monochromatic council of millionaires and billionaires. He stared into their eyes, and he saw the rotten souls which acted as the machine's cold black beating heart, but he did not back down. He warned them that the monster's cloak had fallen away and the people all saw it for what it was- and how they now understood their power in its presence. He told them the people were ready to stop feeding themselves to the machine in order to let it die so that a new world could be built from its best scraps, and he told the council his words were promise not threat.

The rich old white men of the council panicked. They offer Bodhi money, more than a lowly No-Cred could possibly ever dream of, enough even to buy his own Kong Kristian house with views of all of those he would cheat out of justice and survival. He refused it.

They offered him the thing most unimaginable to a person of Gypsy birth; power. Not only would he be the only Gypsy allowed to live in White City- though his dwelling would surely be upon a boundary line with the less-lavish H.C. Anderson district, but he was offered seats upon prestigious boards, committees, and councils which helped to shape the city's economic growth. Bodhi knew his role on these boards, committees, and councils would be largely ceremonial, a token minority to add a dash of diversity among the whitewashed upper crust of Viborg City society. His ego would be inflated as his voice was silenced. He refused it.

Bodhi told the old white men, "I will kill your machine, but seek not to hurt you all. We could save the machine, build it into something which could benefit all inhabitants of Viborg City. I seek only equality and fairness, in all things from education to employment to environment, and you men have the power to grant such a wild wish. You are the wizards of White City, and I stand before you seeking change only you can allow."

The council responded by rubbing their chins, scratching their heads, and checking their cellphones. The rich old white men hunched over and covered their mouths as they whispered amongst themselves. While Bodhi waited patiently, granting them far more respect than they truly deserved, a bald man wearing dark sunglasses and an expensive three piece suit silently entered through the large oak boardroom doors behind him and sat a wooden baseball bat against the door frame.

The bald man in the suit slowly pulled on a pair of black gloves and retrieved the bat from where he placed it. The bald man rested the bat on his left shoulder and adjusted his red power tie with his right hand.

"We have your answer, young Gypsy." One of the rich old white men spoke in a defiant voice.

Bodhi smiled at the men, assuming foolishly they had given into reason and goodness, and were prepared to offer up compromises and solutions.

The bald man in the suit smiled as well as he lifted the bat up off his shoulder. He swung it as hard as he could at the back of Bodhi's head. Wood beat against skull, and skull splintered in response.

Bodhi dropped to his knees. The devastating blow had caused a massive hemorrhage and blood ran from his ears, mouth, nose and eyes. His vision went blurry, distorted, but he felt like he was seeing the rich old white men in their true hellish form- demons of pure hate and greed. His mouth moved to form words of protest, words to beg for mercy, but when he tried to speak these words only dark crimson blood issued forth. He lifted his hands from his sides and began praying to the old gods of his clan, and, finally, the words trickled through the blood. He prayed not for mercy or for escape, he prayed to bid greeting to his ancestors of old.

The bald man in the suit lifted his wooden baseball bat up over his head with both hands. He brought it down on the back of Bodhi's head with all his strength. Bodhi's eyes bulged obscenely in their sockets and he flopped to the floor. The bald man in the suit looked to the rich old white man who spoke to Bodhi. The rich old white man nodded, and the bald man in the suit brought his bat down on Bodhi's skull three more times.

The bald man in the suit finished his task, and left the boardroom without a word.

Two other broad-shouldered white men in expensive suits walked in. They nodded to the council, each grabbed Bodhi by his arms or legs and carried him out of the boardroom without a word.

The council pressed a button and summoned two janitors, two Gypsy janitors from Sorgbjerg who were planning to attend the largest labor meeting held there yet, to clean Bodhi's blood and brains and bits of skull from the floor. They did so without a word.

That evening all of the Gypsies in Sorgbjerg were gathered to hear Bodhi speak, to tell them what said the council of their demands. As they stood waiting anxiously, a white van pulled up to the curb. The side door slid open, Bodhi was tossed out onto the sidewalk, and the van pulled away deliberate and slow. The crowd gathered around Bodhi, though each person remained only long enough to see with their own eyes how his skull had been cracked open and how his brains leaked from those jagged fractures. One by one they walked away from his carcass, leaving their hope like grave-side roses as they scampered back to their red brick buildings.

Bodhi, Bodhi the Gypsy, last of his clan to have a traditional birth, chosen one to carry the old ways forward and to awaken old gods and restore prosperity, had his own unique death rites. No members of his clan, or his broader family of Gypsies for that matter, approached his battered corpse. No one pressed their thumbs to his swollen forehead. No one offered ancient traditional blessings. No one offered personal farewells. His corpse was left to rot in the middle of the sidewalk, so afraid were they to touch it and show it the slightest bit of compassion. It turned to bones, decaying day by day, as the people stepped around it as they dragged themselves to and from work, to the store, to school, to their crumbling red brick tenements. Starving stray animals picked his bones apart, spreading his remains to every alley in Sorgbjerg, and the machine that is Viborg City rumbled on.

Dharma of the Dianthus

Chris Kelso

My name is Nab. That's what the people called me when I created the Bellona Dianthus. So far it's my only success.

Christ-Eye is nigh. I'm running out of time. This is my last chance to prove them all wrong. Still, the moving finger writes. Judgment approaches with the drum and pluck of tautened gut-muscles. Gastrointestinal clairvoyance is mine. My intuitive instincts haven't completely evaded me. I suppose that's something.

Already I hate her, the creation I call 'D'. She is only a letter and an idea, yet I hate her inmost being. She is a reflection of me and, I suppose, any perceived lack of depth 'D' might display is a damning indictment of my own flawed character. This kind of scrutiny comes with the territory.

"Can you hear me calling you?"—I ask her deep within myself.

The void replies with silence.

I peer hard into imaginary eyes, two dismal pools of glittering semen, and witness *nothing* staring back at me, *nothing*. Glazed television screens stuck on a dead channel; even from this Black Throne on high I feel the shallowness of insipid waters. Maybe they're right about me? I will gaze upon this chequer-board of Nights and Days with no instruments of victory, a eunuch. There is no new strategy.

"Fill this paper with the breathings of my heart... *please...*"—I say to her.

Still nothing.

There needs to be poetry present, you see. I can't afford another failure, unfortunately I have never been much of a poet. *Remember*, I say to myself, *even Omar Khayyám managed to perfect his Rubaiyat verses over nine centuries!* I take some solace in this but I'm nothing if not realistic.

Journalists will say I am afflicted with empty palms, fingertips void of soul-giving. What do they know? They're all so quick to judge me. Can I help it if the precious opiate of life eludes me? I must keep trying. The journalists and debunkers can't win. Surely there is even less poetry in a cynic prevailing.

Mid-mould, the audio display rings in a refrain of '*La cucaracha*'—Mex Harpo. Of all the people, why'd it have to be him? That overstuffed clack-box of a man...

I pick up the receiver, place it to my ear and hear Harpo's breathless hunger emerge in distorted surges of barbed static. I can almost picture him on the other line, standing erect, like a parody of the stale, smelly beaurocrat. All awkward angles and perma-tan. The opposite of my aged, sagging body.

"How are you Mr One-Hit Wonder? Any luck with the Christ-Eye? Still as cow handed as ever?"

"Not that it's any of your business but..."

"Ha, alright Nab, well that'll be *no* luck then?"—He snorts. I can make out the contracted muscles of a shit-eating grin form as he mocks me. Can virtually smell the expensive cinched suit of untanned seal-skin.

"Gladstone was right about you. The Christ-Eye gets bloodshot in a matter of hours. Your god status is hanging by..."

"Never you mind my god status you fustilarian gnash-gab!"—My insult gains only a derisory whinny from Harpo. Particles of carbon and water spear the air in front of me like abstractions of flight. I can feel my creative energy sapped under the scrutiny of this man.

I move to hang up the audio display but that would be conceding defeat. I keep him on the line, tense my fist around the ear-piece until the plastic makes a crack. I decide to give him a piece of my mind.

"You journalists are all the same, aren't you, Harpo?"

"Are we?"

"You're all just failed, bitter architects who gave up trying to craft life with your mind. The Christ-Eye scares you! Don't ever forget that, you're a sad little nobody."

There is a moments silence before his hideous belly-laugh blasts down the receiver. I watch the falcate moonlets of Cindra descend and blush, turning the sky a hue of bloody red that's surely befitting of my inevitable fate at the hands of Gladstone. My old body needs acceptance to be young again. Even the acceptance of Mex Harpo.

"If I gave up on trying to create life then that makes me a realist. I found out early I wasn't a soul-giver so I got a new occupation, and I'm bloody good at investigative journalism. You, well, *you* can't take a hint!"

A journalist? *Hardly.*

I suppose Mex Harpo is considered a celebrity of sorts, but ultimately he is a huckster of tabloid trash. At the time of our initial introduction Harpo was not a journalist but a debunker of religious charlatans and phonies on behalf of the state. The swine chased me for months hoping a high profile exposé would elevate his résumé to the Gilded-Standard of the Cindra Assembly of Demystification. It took my creation of Cindra's inert vapour (emitted from a redundant flower called the Bellona Dianthus: a plant which sustains itself on the steady streams of sugar water passing through the region)--*my only useful creation to date*—to subdue Harpo's interest in me. As a journalist he is no less the shameless careerist.

"Why are you so obsessed with what I'm up to anyway?"

"It's my job. You use a lot of taxpayer money to fund your creative environment. You don't have long is all I'm saying. I'm looking for some freelance case-work in Demystification, they more or less begged me to come back to the Assembly. A few high profile cases exposing preeminent leaders and transcendentalist charlatans will bring in some extra credits. I never did debunk you though, did I? Bet you thought I'd moved on, let you off the hook? You've ridden on the back of that fart-smelling Bellona Dianthus gas long enough. You got lucky."

"Luck has nothing to do with it! I willed it!"

"Luck has everything to do with it! Maybe you've seen me in the Cindra Argus lately? If not, I can usually be spotted, centre-page, apprehending some self-proclaimed Mahatma on the steps of his spiritual hermitage. I never give up on something if it's not beyond me. See you at the city for your press junket. I'll be there in a journalistic capacity, don't worry."

Harpo gives one last condescending cackle before disconnecting the call. I return to my work, flustered and distracted. Waves of blowtorched heat waft across my aperture. The Christ-Eye is almost inflamed. A new thirst seizes me, ploughing deep furrows into my throat and the vulnerability of my humanity makes me balk. The Christ-Eye orbits so close to land that the exoplanet becomes tidally locked, temporarily-- water is hard to come by, even the sugar water beneath the soil is only good for cooking with. Fortunately, for now at least, I have God-Status. The disturbed warmth bites into my skin so I fill a bowl with a ladleful of ambrosia and sup its froth from around the lip. It swamps the dryness in my throat. Lets the devil in, relaxes the body.

Focus…

★★★

At this stage, 'D' is simply stardust-- swirling atoms observed and lusted after through the objective lens of my microscope. She has never committed a carnal sin, this one. Her embryonic innocence intimidates me and the heart's woes are legion.

I near my face to the ghost of hers. My nostrils echo on the exhale the closer I get.

I draw in her hair. Dogwood blossom. Skin smells of baking soda, the cosmetic scent of iris and galbanum. She is ready in the minds-eye. I call for the waters of the sea and pour them out over the face of the land, the contours of her beautiful physiognomy reveal themselves. *Yes…*

I've done well with the external work, I usually do. She looks good. Starry host by the breath of my mouth. I anoint her with the pressed sap of nectar. My old body heaves her into the physical world.

Eventually, she achieves consciousness and the strewn ramparts of her cells start to communicate on a metabolic level, debating structure and projection. Her physical body forms before me like a too-real fever dream. Silverbright pupils hang in the low-light from the flickering, fluorescent overhang. I willed this. Now I have to finish the job properly.

I probe around, trying to find the ON switch. It's not long before I discover that she can't be turned on. *Shit! Not again!* Her flesh cannot meet the electricity of life--this pink blancmange of want and inevitable loss. I have surely failed once more. Harpo's condemnations ring in my ear like the final bugle call before a military execution. What did Gladstone say about me exactly?

Blood orange suns meet outside, and are immediately eclipsed by the Christ-eye. High clouds laced with silicate particles. I'm out of time. Once again I've focused too much on her external beauty. Nary a day goes by that I don't curse my quest for physical perfection. But I need to grant her depth, increase her emotional capacity. I can't burn out with the reputation of a glorified mannequin-maker! Only the spectacle of the Christ-eye escapes my dissatisfaction.

Time to walk into the lion's den. I take 'D' by the hand and set off across the graphite valleys and recessed wens to the urban ashrams of Cindra's holy philosophers. She says nothing on the way and the empty storefront window of her gaze barely succeeds in penetrating the air in front of her. Nothing insightful surfaces for the entire duration of our journey.

★★★

I long to have my lifework described as a surrealist prose performance, full of success and catastrophe—my notes studied as a series of internal Socratic debates punctuated by self-defining arias. I would love to be a Joycean God but that is something else I cannot simply will.

We stand before a press junket, naked, sweating, awaiting a verdict. She goes to open her mouth but only inane platitudes fall out—"My hobbies include hanging out with girlfriends and I hope to meet a nice rich boy one day, settle down and get married." The collective groan of the holy men, field marshalls, archbishops, and journalists erupts like pent up wind and shakes the teardrops from thine eyes. Mex Harpo is there too, grinning. Like this is the last evidence he needed before pulling the plug on my whole operation. His mop of shaggy, unkempt hair rises in the static and gives him a blonde halo.

We depart the foyer to a hail of blinking camera bulbs, lights like knives. I'm sure she feels her first rejection. How could she not? She is just a letter, not much more.

There are departing prosecutions of *'Clichéd'*, *'Shallow'*, and *'Forgettable'* that catch in the chest where pride is situated. I hear someone call me 'a puffed up botanist!'

I cannot deny these claims. The Christ-Eye weeps its jewels. My body ages another ten years.

Of course, the press unanimously deem her insufficient and so we make the long return trip saturated in the residue of failure. I won't be looking at the front page tomorrow.

★★★

On the gurney her lips bloom from the blank mud like silver lotuses and I can't resist meeting with her in a kiss. Even though I hate her more than ever. I place a second kiss upon her brow, salting my lips with the flavour of epithelium. I've travelled to the Thules of this world, drank from its lone waters. Nothing has helped me recreate the sentient spirit. I am a master of the sun-bleached hair and honey skinned girl. The fart smelling gas. Not much else.

The audio display rings—*la cucaracha*. I choose to ignore it.

"Isn't that the phone?"—D asks expressionlessly, my lip-mark still impressed upon her forehead. If only I could kiss her heart.

"Yes, but listen…what do you want from this life?"—I clench my fists to illustrate desire, clench until the fingers crack in my palm and a bead of ichor seeps from a ruptured vein.

"Want?"—The audio display ceases its refrain and the girl's eyes go wide and birdshot around the lower lid. Has she just come online?

"Yes! Tell me something. Anything. There must be a glimmer of humanity beneath those subcutaneous layers of beauty."

She takes a moment and I hear the gears in her head grinding together to form an authentic thought. She shifts on the gurney and looks at me.

"A name, I'd like a name. Not a letter. Something I can say to cute men when I first meet them."

She wants a name, which means she's conscious of some internal search for an identity.

"How about…Dianthus after my masterpiece."

"How about Diane?"

"Perfect!"

A little common, basic, unoriginal maybe, but we must proceed in baby steps. I could still lose her.

"I'm naked."—She notes.

"Yes, you are."

Self-awareness! Shame.

"I'd like some clothes."

I conjure a blanket for her shivering body.

"Any sugar water?"

"Yes, I'll get you some soon."

I realise that a creature of nature will be blessed with emotional acuity because she is connected to everything and everyone who has gone before. I think about those inert emissions which secreted from the Bellona Dianthus. Why change a winning formula?

"I have a better idea--I tell her--Something that will help us both."

★★★

Diane is almost there, almost sentient—a true miracle in the absence of the Christ-Eye. One more push should do it. I conjure enough plant material to protect her fragile clay, to wrap her organs in the stupendous and cosmogonal philosophy of the Bhagvad Geeta. Her roots may be in art and magic but she is one with the blanched soil, damp and eternal. Diane now has the tonic of wilderness in her blood. People will come to envy her. She will be the most perfect example of a living person. Mex Harpo will beg my forgiveness.

I increase her half-life to $RCln(2)$ and send electrical impulses to the forearm through the skin. Her muscles contract, and then the movement begins. Finally, I call her a cunt and she recoils from my arms.

"A cunt?"—She winces.

Sensitivity. It worked. Introspection should come next.

Releasing her into my paradisiac garden is a moving scene. Diane attacks the landscape with an immigrants love, disappearing into the wild ferns and I see her frolicking bare-foot through long, lush unmowed grass. I am witnessing something truly poignant. Returning an animal to its natural habitat, or, rather, its adopted habitat.

★★★

I look out my aperture and see Diane washing my smooth-leaved plants with a moist, soft cloth and some insecticidal soap. She is so delicate and loving that I cannot bear to call her back into the house for a final test. But I must.

She comes in and greets me with a peaceful smile.

"Diane, have you noticed any changes in your perspective lately?"

She tilts her head and really considers the gravity of my question.

"For one, I don't want cute men, well, not *just* cute men. I want something of substance, to read and learn and affect things. There is no longer any desire for money and I'm aware of a growing aversion to the notion of war."

"Good. And, do you have goals or motivations?"

"I want to return somewhere, the place I belong"

"You mean... my imagination?"

"No, I think I have graduated beyond a two dimensional, half-realised character in a bad short story. I want to go to where the plants live, underground. I long for mulch and to provide sustenance for insects. I think this would give me tremendous peace and happiness, to give myself to the creatures of the Christ-Eye."

Incredible. She really has become something quite unique. I swell with a maternal pride and concern. Then it occurs to me that I can't let her go. Not just yet.

"You can't return to the soil Diane my beautiful creature. You don't belong there."

Even as the words come out of my mouth I know how

unreasonable they must sound. The girl looks at me as a swarm of fungus gnats appear in her palm and bury their way beneath the strata of loam and flesh.

"But…"

"Come with me to the Cindra ashrams one more time. Just so I can show everyone that you were a success. Please. Then we'll work on returning you to the Great Mother. It's the right thing to do for the living things in this world, and those trying to achieve life."

She accepts. Her eyes are warm, selfless, burning with compassion and a lust to do the right thing for her planet. She is fantastic, everything I would hope for from my children. Already she seems to have exceeded me in every way. But then one must not forget about the Steppenwolf, a being both man and wolf. When Herman Hesse talked about the Steppenwolf, he was denoting the duality of man and the various souls inherent to one body. I too am a man of many souls. Diane's goodness must reside in me somewhere. After all, she is a direct reflection of me.

★★★

Through a sheet of gauzy pollen, a congregation of wild animals stand to attention.

In Cindra, Diane sits beside me deliberating the effect of fossil fuel consumption and viable alternative energy resources with the head of the Cindra Ecological Assemblage. He seems quite impressed with her suggestions that we extract solar energy from the Christ-Eye using solar thermal or photovoltaic cells. Things couldn't be going more according to plan.

A man appears beside me, bull-necked, strapping—it's Thelonious Apesift, an MP in possession of considerable renown and social standing in Cindra. He has long wavy hair and crescent-shaped sunburn from the Christ-Eye across his forehead. He forwards his meaty hand and connects with mine in a shake. My wrist flops in his grasp like a wilted petunia.

"Straight to it then Nab. Does your creation have any political opinions?"

"Oh yes, she is staunchly anti-war and imbued with a self-shaped theistic bhakti that would make most monastery goers rear their heads in shame. To think the missing ingredients were the same plant-based ingredients I used to conjure gas from a small, docile, indigenous plant!"

Apesift looks at me through suspicious eyes. Diane leaves a conversation with the health minister to add—

"I believe our identity politics polarize us. Also, Politicians are intrinsically corrupt and I refuse to have any opinions one way or the other. Does that answer your question?"

Apesift nods, a little stunned and reverses himself back into the crush of journalists.

"Be seeing you Thelonious."

"Can I trouble you for a glass of sugar water?"—Diane asks.

"Of course. When we're done here I'll get you some."

I see a bald dome shift passage through the active crowd towards me. It can only be Fairfield Merriweather, gossip columnist. He's around a foot taller than anyone else in the room so it's a fair assumption to make. When Merriweather eventually reaches me his face is awash with sweat. He can barely get out the gossip he's painstakingly travelled so far to deliver. I give him a moment.

"They're saying you're God Status is cemented. They're saying…"—he struggles to catch a breath. My patience wanes.

"What, what are they saying?"

"They're saying…that you're going to be the next big deity."

"Really?"

"Yes, they want to ship you out to Ursa Minor where they're simply crying out for a new god to worship after the Salt Wars devastated their crops."

"That's…amazing."

"I hurried over here as soon as the story was corroborated by Gladstone himself."

"The news came from Gladstone?"

"Yes. He says he admires your boldness. No one has ever come back for a press junket after such a huge bomb."

"Well, that is a compliment."

I take in the balsams, the smoky ozone, and feel calmed. Pride soon takes over. My mind runs amok, I already envisage myself as the saviour of lowly little Ursa Minor. I need to find Mex Harpo, after all, he's the whole reason I came back to the Cindra ashrams. I scan the room and spot the editor from Harpo's scandal sheet the Cindra Argus talking to a group of senior military men. Among the faces in the clutch of parasites, I see Harpo's bloated, pompous visage. I can barely stop myself moving in his direction, I'm possessed by a gloating, vengeful spirit. He sees me coming and mutters something under his breath. I interrupt a conversation between Commander Haggles and a cocky young Argus intern whose name has escaped me.

"So, Harpo…"

"Yes, yes…"

"Do you still think I'm just a 'child playing with big boy toys'?"

Harpo looks at his editor and frowns.

"I suppose…I…"

"Yes? You suppose…?"

Just as the longed-for expression of regret emerges in a huffed, reluctant breath, I hear a strange noise coming from the stage. A blinding ovular light forms in the sky. I turn and see Diane making harsh choking sounds. Everyone has gathered around her, seemingly concerned, but not concerned in the way a living thing feels toward another living thing—more like the way a child panics when a toy robot starts to malfunction. A plume of gas emerges from Diane's mouth and the crowd back away holding their noses.

The Christ-Eye looms above, blinks once, and Cindra is completely enveloped in its ghostly mantle. Diane starts falling about, green-tinted vapour belching forth and rising into the air in a churning maelstrom.

"What's going on?"—I hear Harpo asking me.

"I don't know…Diane!"

The smell, only I could make that smell.

Diane, still wheezing, tears open her kaftan, revealing, to a chorus of gasps, two taut breasts unto the holy mob. Her nipples tighten into hard beads and Governess Neon Wyncote faints into the arms of her husband Ajax.

"What kind of atrocity is this?"—Thelonious Apesift demands, outraged.

My first instinct is to rush over to Diane, throw a robe around her shoulders and get her as far away from this audience of judgemental leeches and bespawling triptakers as possible, but I stop myself from entering the spotlight. Whatever foul thing is happening to Diane right now, it's something inherent to her genetic make-up, a necessary stage in the core principles of being I instilled in her. I cannot interfere. A god cannot interfere. The Cindra crowd will have their way with me eventually.

"Look!"—I hear Mex Harpo shout above the abominable din of my faulty creation.

The Christ-Eye sits, bloodshot and vein-streaked, like a monolith on the tallest hill eclipsing the horseshoe moonlets. With one shuddering blink it casts a solid beam of focused light onto Diane's writhing body, setting her instantly aflame. My gut wrenches the way any mothers gut must wrench at the sight of her child's demise. Diane crumbles and cracks, soil pours forth from her dermis until she is reduced to a pile of reeking compost stacked next to Pen Gladstone's feet. He stares at me through the crowd with antipathy in his gaze. Everything is faintly aglow with the tangerine orange of Diane's flames.

"What is the meaning of this?"—Gladstone asks and the crowd all crane their necks to face me in livid expectancy.

"It is the personal dharma of the plant to provide oxygen, to fertilise and provide for the surrounding environment. Not to be paraded and questioned on matters of politics."

Diane, the creation I used to despise, is the recipient of a truly merciful act.

Now that the best part of me has been eviscerated I'm left with my audience and my shame. The burning sphere in the sky creases its lids and begins a slow descent.

My head feels heavy with soil. I no longer have the capacity for hate. I suppose there is solace in this also. After today there will be no more damning indictments.

Mirrors, Cities

Vincenzo Bilof

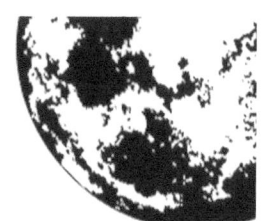

Detective Prior popped his collar and stuffed his hands into his jacket. *At least I look like a detective,* he thought as he surveyed the crime scene.

"I think this guy was NoCred," his partner, Miles, said. You could count on Miles to touch shit all over the crime scene with ungloved hands. Tonight, he was eating a ham sandwich and getting crumbs on the hardwood floor in the apartment.

"Okay," Prior said. He peered down at the corpse. It was his way. Miles didn't care one way or the other. The detectives were experts at tolerating each other.

"Name's Carlo Bialer," Miles said as if the whole process was an inconvenience. "He, uh, he sold books, or rented books."

"Rented books?"

"Guy's a NoCred. Owns a lot of books."

The small room in the NoCred apartment building was stuffed with bookshelves, stacks of dusty tomes piled on the floor because the shelves themselves were overcrowded. The room smelled like dust and cats.

Another non-crime, Prior thought. *They justify keeping me just because of Irene.*

"So, a heart attack, right?" Miles said with his mouth full.

"That's what they said."

"Cool. I'm going to head out, grab a beer. Or five."

"Yup," Prior said.

"We supposed to write it up?"

"I'll have it done in the morning."

This game has to end sometime, Prior thought.

Miles walked out, leaving Detective Prior in a room full of books and a dead man. He spent another three minutes not looking around, decided he had been there too long, and left.

★★★

Prior unbuckled his pants, lay them out on the bed, looked at them. Loose, black dress pants. They were loose seven years ago. *Time for new ones,* he thought, and then remembered the graphics upgrade he needed for the computer.

They'll be comfortable tomorrow. He watched his wife coming out of the bathroom, her underwear older than his.

"Going to bed," Anna said.

"I have a report to write," he said.

I'm not writing a report.

"Okay," she said.

He walked into the living room in shorts and a shirt. He fired up the computer, heard the fan buzz more loudly than it should have. *I might as well treat myself.* He thought. *Not getting any younger.* The South-East China models were all the rage because they were smaller, faster. Some wondered if the sudden legality of the enemy tech was because they were winning the war, and some wondered if they could use the tech because they were losing the war and the South-East Chinese had infiltrated them; in reality they had already lost the war but hadn't been officially told.

Prior didn't care either way.

Buying the latest computer would set him back a lot. There was a chance his rent would be late by a whole month if he bought the computer, and his Cred had been extended and the payments spread out longer for a new jacket he bought himself—a jacket he still hadn't worn.

He was close, now. Close to asking the city for a loan.

Instead of logging onto Erewhon to solve pretend homicides, he began typing up a report from the evening.

★★★

He began his report:

I am still employed out of a sense of loyalty from someone, or because they know I will be desperate enough to do a desperate and dangerous thing for them at some point. They know I will say yes because I will want to save my marriage. I will want to feel as if I am married. And I can imagine a nice South-East China machine with the fastest processor possible, or faster. They know I will take the job. They will know I won't have a choice.

I am still employed because they want to watch me. They like Irene, or they hate Irene. They are obsessed with her.

A man had died of a heart attack and two detectives were dispatched to the scene. There is nothing to report. That is the point. That's why we were sent. We do nothing but confirm there is nothing more to say.

He deleted the entire report, logged into Erewhon.

★★★

In Erewhon, his avatar is a tall Arab woman named Irene, and she solves homicides. She is not perturbed by the sight of blood. She has a stunning reputation, almost mythic in forums and messageboards. Irene made the news in the reality world. People wanted to meet her. People wanted to know who the real person was behind the avatar. And the press loved to speculate. She was used to investigate assassinations and corporate murders. She became a sort of television show; the government had hired expert programmers to enact plotlines that required Irene's involvement.

Prior wanted a real assignment.

He did not want to be Irene anymore. When he logged on, he stared at Irene for a minute, logged off.

There would probably be a phone call tomorrow. A recording of a summary of critical events that happened in Erewhon. There would be a veiled hint, and a veiled threat. Get your ass back to Erewhon and be Irene. Maybe you don't wake up tomorrow.

★★★

There was no phone call. He woke up, made coffee, said hello to Anna. Put on the pants he'd worn yesterday after inspecting them for wrinkles and stains. He opened his closet and put on the jacket he had worn yesterday. A gray, wooly affair. Cheap.

He drove to the office. Said hello to a few people, gritted his teeth for the sake of fake smiles, walked to this desk and sat down. It wasn't a minute before Miles sat down across from him.

"Hey asshole, I need that report," Miles said.

"There is nothing to report."

"We were out. Do something. Give us credit for showing up."

"I was about to."

"You fucked up. These other guys don't know who you are. You transferred in, made a habit of being nothing and doing nothing. But you're the guy who didn't catch Ole, from the Potemkin Crew. I mean, they found him, but you didn't. These other guys don't know."

"Tell them. They can't do anything worse to me. Like you said. I got habits."

Miles got up, shook his head. Left.

Prior sat in his chair. Fell asleep for a little bit. He didn't dream.

When he woke up, there was a memo on his desk. A question about his report.

Which books?

Detective Prior stared at it for a few moments and didn't think much about it. He looked around the office for Miles. *Probably went home. And he had to bring up Ole. Lean on me, then, Miles. You think you're watching me, but you're really watching Irene.*

He left the office and drove back to the apartment where he had stood over a dead man who had a heart attack yesterday. There was crime scene tape over the apartment door. For a man who had a heart attack.

Irene wouldn't rip it up, he thought about his famous avatar. *A useless gesture.*

The detective had to remove the top layer of tape barring the door, then stretched himself slowly and uncomfortably over the rest of the tape.

He turned on the lights in the apartment, walked into the bedroom where Carlo had died alone.

And then he thought about the question on the memo. *Which books?*

Someone knew he was desperate, knew he wanted a real case. Miles could have been screwing with him, but the guy wasn't all that vindictive. The note could have been left on his desk accidentally by someone walking by. But here he was. He had driven to the NoCred apartment because deep down, he needed the note to mean something.

He scanned the spines of old, unjacketed books. He recognized one, because he had read it during the investigation that landed him in Purgatory: *The Potemkin Overture*. The story of the legendary hacker crew. Markus, Ole, Nick.

Not a coincidence, he thought and grabbed the book. *It's time. I'm back in the game.*

★★★

Prior took the book home and thought about what he would have to do as Irene. It was going to be a long night. When he got home, he told Anna that he would be on the computer. His words implied it would be for a lengthy period of time. She did not look at him when he said it.

He logged on and stared at Irene for a bit.

He logged off and began re-reading *The Potemkin Overture*. Anna did not talk to him the rest of the night; she was reading a book in bed and he did not look at the cover, did not ask her what it was about.

"Can we watch something?" he asked her.

"The remote's next to you," she said.

Of course it is, he thought. He turned on a show about a Cash family. He watched them go shopping. There were two teenage girls in the family. Both of them were drastically different, though both were blonde, as blonde as everything else in Viborg City. The girls had an argument about something. When Anna eventually fell asleep, Prior put the book down and went to the computer. He logged in, stared at Irene, logged off.

★★★

Instead of going to the office in the morning, he went to the most important NoCred apartment building in the city. There was a good chance his old friend would be around during the day.

Even in the NoCred part of the city, the streets were clean.

It wasn't like this in places such as St. Petersburg. Life wouldn't be all that bad if they had to move. Maybe Anna would like it. Maybe there would be no pressure in their lives. Maybe they could talk to each other. Maybe they could put more effort into acknowledging that the other existed. It might be better to starve together in desperation. It might be like holding each other while on fire.

He made it to the apartment, knocked on the door, thought for a second about Miles. *Call me an asshole and ask for the report. He's getting angrier by the second. He'll tell someone, try to kick my ass a bit. He's got nothing better to do.* Some men just need a reason to breathe.

An old man named Dr. Sojo opened the door.

"*Amigo*, I hope you can make this quick."

"You don't remember me?"

"That's why I don't want to talk. Of course I remember you."

"No, I mean I really need your help. What you specialize in."

"I've answered all the questions," Dr. Sojo said.

"Just a minute of your time. For me, personally."

Dr. Sojo sighed. *Used to always have a big smile,* Prior thought. The long beard was no longer white, but gray, dusty. One of the most respectable connections to the best hallucinogenic drug in town, SYNTH. It wasn't a secret. There were no mysteries behind Dr. Sojo, mostly because people stopped asking. Prior had banked on the fact that the doctor was a lonely old man with nothing to do, nowhere to go.

here used to be a ton of books and a fantastic collection of punk rock albums inside Dr. Sojo's apartment. They had been sold or stolen after Viborg City cracked down on Synth. The place was empty. Not even the dust wanted to stay here.

The Jihad flag still hung over the bedroom door.

They sat on Arab stools apart from each other. Prior opened up his jacket because he was warm. Dr. Sojo peered at him through big glasses.

"I guess I'll just come out with it."

"Sure, *amigo*," Dr. Sojo said.

"I don't know who my avatar is. I have developed a really

complex personality, and I don't know who she is anymore. I'm not having nightmares about it or anything."

"You're talking about Erewhon."

"Yeah. I told you I genuinely want help."

"You need your avatar right now?"

"I think so. I think I used to need it, badly."

"Badly? Man, this is out of my league. I mostly collected data. When I made conclusions about the data they said get out and take your shit with you."

"You're talking about SYNTH."

"You want some?"

"A long time ago. It's actually easy for me to say no."

"You didn't get it directly from me."

"Maybe that's what happened."

Dr. Sojo coughed again.

"So what I'm saying is I can't help you. You want a head doctor. They'll put your ass in Kronberg, won't even ask too many questions about it, either."

Detective Prior thought for a moment. "I was here a few times. You must have seen a lot of people. Or maybe I'm just an ugly guy."

Dr. Sojo coughed through a bout of laughter. "Shit. I thought you had come here to kill me. Maybe you still have. You going to kill me?"

"Why would I do that?"

"I don't know. I don't know why anyone does anything. You said your personality has been disassociated. Why would I be an expert?"

"You made SYNTH."

Wrong button. Dr. Sojo's jaw clenched and he stared at the detective. His head seemed to be trembling, the wiry remains of his hair shaking.

"Made SYNTH," the old man said. "That's what you think?"

"You worked for the government, right? They wanted you to test it."

"You're a fool. You'll believe anything. What if I told you it's in the water supply? What if I told you that you're logged on right now, to Erewhon, and the avatar you think you have is actually the real you."

Prior laughed. "OK. I just meant since you knew what SYNTH could do, you could maybe help me with this problem I've got. My avatar is kind of important, not just to me, but to a lot of people."

"You got the wrong guy."

"It was the only thing I looked forward to. The only way I could justify working a shitty job."

"You need a friend, not a doctor. Or if you need a doctor, you need a specialist."

"You are the specialist. You know all about different realities."

"*Amigo,* I think this is where I tell you to go fuck yourself."

"Just tell me what's wrong with me."

"Yeah. Sorry I can't help you. I would if I could. Really, I got nothing else to do."

The detective removed a book from his jacket and passed it to Dr. Sojo.

"Something for you to do," Prior said. "I've read it before. You've probably read it before, too. It was popular for a little while. I actually just read it again. You ever meet Ole, or Markus Olsen?"

"I've read the book."

"I'm trying to solve a crime," Detective Prior said.

"You, or your avatar?"

"Both of us."

"You said it was a she. Humor me, *amigo,* why a girl?"

"Is it important to know why? A lot of people choose the opposite gender, or no gender."

"It could be important."

"Why don't you take down your Jihad flag?"

"Stay awhile, *amigo.*"

★★★

Which books?

Detective Prior had never talked about Irene with his wife, Anna. He assumed Anna just knew and didn't say anything, or she wouldn't care if he told her. Now, Dr. Sojo knew the identity behind his avatar.

Irene had sex and maintained relationships with men. Irene accepted awards. Irene had dinner with politicians.

And now, she was missing.

He returned to the apartment where Carlo had died and attempted to scour the bookshelves. He didn't know what he was looking for. *Which books?*

Inside the room where he had found a dead man, he sat on the edge of the bed. *I should at least know who this man was.* He roamed around the apartment, opened drawers. *Why did you have so many books, Carlo? How did you pay for them? Why didn't you sell them to collectors? Who would choose to be a NoCred?*

And then, a more disturbing thought: *I am a detective, and I was sent here to stare at a dead man and write a report. There is no crime. There is no case. There is nothing. But there are books.*

Where should he start? Another familiar book, maybe?

I am desperate for a case. The note was probably shit, probably meant nothing.

He returned to the books, began to scan the titles again.

Dr. Sojo had eventually talked, had said that Irene is nothing more than the person he wants to be. His death in the real worlds kills both of them. Dr. Sojo made that point clear: if Detective Prior dies, Irene dies. Only one of the two lives is real. Decide which one it is.

But: *Which book?*

The True Story of Olgey Tazar, obviously.

The story of a poet who had been a hacker, once. The story of a dead man. The story of a man who had eluded Detective Prior. The story of Ole, who had become Olgey Tazar, the famous poet of Samarqand.

The book did not have an author.

What am I trying to do? he wondered. He had created his own investigation. There was no investigation. There was no crime. These books would be in any man's library, even if they were a NoCred. These books could have belonged to Dr. Sojo at one point. The fact that he had picked up a book from the shelf last time was purely coincidental, unrelated to anything. He should not have visited Dr. Sojo. The old man had people he wanted to impress, because he was desperate and probably a junkie. Dr. Sojo might have the backing of serious Cash.

And the writing styles between the two books—as Prior flipped through the book, he thought the writing styles were similar. Olgey Tazar—Ole—might have written *The Potemkin Overture*, and may have written *The True Story of Olgey Tazar*. Or Ole had not written either of them. Somebody else had written them.

I don't know what I'm doing here, Prior thought. *And nobody can tell me what I am doing here. Who is the man who had lived here? Who was this man who had died in a room in which a crime was not committed?*

He grabbed the book and drove to the office.

★★★

"Why were you at Dr. Sojo's?" Miles asked.

Detective Prior sat behind his desk. "Why are you asking?"

"I got a job to do, buddy."

"You know about me, but I don't know about you."

"How long we been working together?" Miles asked.

"We haven't worked together. Not once."

Miles laced his fingers behind his head and leaned back. "You back on SYNTH?"

"I wish. People began to superimpose reality upon a dream, I think, when they were on it. I didn't get that far. I messed around with it."

"Is that why you didn't catch Ole?"

"I didn't find him because he decided to become a poet. Think about it: who in their right mind retires from hacker life to write poetry?"

Miles whistled. "I bet that part doesn't matter. He wasn't killed in Viborg City. The Western Alliance wasn't threatened because of how it went down. He died a poet. You were supposed to find a hacker."

"A terrorist," Detective Prior added.

Miles stood. A smell rose with him, cheap hand soap smell because he had washed himself recently, and cheap soap smells clearly on a man who has not washed for a while. Prior had never thought about Miles as being frugal, or possibly a NoCred.

"You ever read Tazar's poems?" Miles asked.

"Never had time."

"Me neither. Anyway, that report."

"What was the guy's name? The corpse."

"What corpse?"

Miles smirked, and his stare lingered an uncomfortable while.

"OK," Detective Prior said.

★★★

At home that evening, Detective Prior read the book and decided he was glad Ole hadn't known he even existed. Ole knew he was being pursued, but had no idea who the hunters were. Maybe he had succeeded at something?

The book was short, but it still took him late into the evening. He didn't sleep. When he finally put the book down, he tried to imagine the dreams Irene would have. What dreams does a fake persona have? The book had been mostly nothing but literary criticism, with zero indictment of his comrades in the Potemkin Crew. Olgey Tazar had imagined himself a literary hero, which was a predictable course of thinking when it came to terrorists. Political criminals believe themselves martyrs to the end. Prior should have been reading books when he was pursuing Ole. He should have been reading for the utmost display of vanity. Seek the men who would be martyrs. Poets, of course, are self-styled martyrs; some connection to pain and suffering is inherent in the definition of those who chronicle the lives of the NoCreds.

And Irene knows how to talk to the NoCreds. What crime is she investigating? Was there a crime? Is there a report to write?

But Irene wasn't investigating a crime. He could not be her. He did not even think about the logging on; the book reminded him of the pursuit, the case that had buried his career, dropped him into detective limbo. Prior worked whatever shit cases they gave him, and they only kept him around because he was good at typing reports. And Irene? Irene was important to Erewhon. The government needed to be there just as much as it needed to be in Viborg City.

He should have asked Dr. Sojo for SYNTH. Why did he turn it down? Idiot. Maybe he could have forgotten this whole affair; write the report, keep saving money for the East China CPU, solve homicides in the virtual world as a virtual woman.

Dr. Sojo couldn't help him with his personal problem, but there was more than one personal problem. Just like there had been more than one person in the Potemkin Crew. More than one hacker-terrorist.

ext morning, Prior skipped coffee, was out of the house an hour earlier than usual. He began the long drive to the prison, and wasn't sure his wife had been in bed with him last night.

He wanted to tell Anna: *Remember the youth we had? The courage? Remember the love we felt for each other? I think I died when I lost Ole. I think I died, and I have tried to live again. I want you to know me. I want someone to know me…*

Carlo, a man who rented books, was dead. There was no investigation.

And he could not be Irene.

But there was a man in a prison who had been someone else.

He arrived at the prison in the early afternoon. Detective Prior had to introduce himself to prison security as such. Official business. They weren't surprised when he inquired about a prisoner. Nothing should be too surprising about this investigation.

here is no investigation.

he prisoner was already in an interview room with a two-way mirror. The interview would be monitored closely, of course. The prisoner didn't stand. His beard was dark, neatly-trimmed. No other markings on his face. His hair was tidy.

"Who are you?" the prisoner asked. "I'm not officially alive."

"You remember who I am," Detective Prior sat down.

"Either I don't know what year it is, or you have aged quickly," Nick said.

"Possibly a little of both."

"I mean, you're the only person outside this prison who thinks I'm alive."

"I'm sure there are others. Your friend Ole became a poet. Wrote about you."

"A poet?"

"Nobody told you."

"You came here to tell me that?"

"You were in his book, Nick."

"That's hard to believe. Ole was quiet, never said shit. Can I go back to my cell?"

Detective Prior pulled the book from his jacket, placed it on the table. He pointed to it. "Ole wrote this. Anyway, I brought it for you. I already cleared it with security. They're going to let you have it. I need a favor from you."

The famous hacker stared at the book for a long time. "I don't have anyone to talk to. That's what you were betting on."

"Come on. That wouldn't be fair. I want you to have the book. If you don't want to help me, I'll leave."

"What? Tell me what it is. I don't know anything about Markus Olsen. Don't ask about Olsen."

"In Erewhon. You have a job there? They put you to work. They wouldn't waste your talents."

Nick looked around the room, then at the ceiling. "You know I don't regret it. I'm not expendable. And goddamn them, I've tried. You know I've tried to do it to myself. End it. But I would do it all over again, only we would do it better. We would succeed. That's how much I hate these people."

"I didn't mean to upset you."

"What is it? What do you want? You want to talk about Erewhon?"

"I have a persona. A popular one. I've spent a lot of time on my avatar. But now I want to retire it."

Nick looked around the room. The former hacker said, "You know what SYNTH is?"

"Of course."

"Ole used to say there was a better way to merge realities. Said they would find it. That they would find it before anyone in Samarqand. The Western Alliance wants to win a war that's probably not even happening, and they're giving you Erewhon, and they're giving you hope. You ever meet a soldier? A real soldier? Someone who's been to the front?"

Detective Prior stood.

"Wait," Nick said. "I asked about SYNTH for a reason. It causes… merge isn't the right word. It's like SYNTH is a water bottle on a kitchen counter. The world is the kitchen counter. There is a hole in the bottle… "

Detective Prior waited. *He is not insane. He is damaged. And they are using him. He's probably an intelligence officer in Erewhon. He would know about Irene, has probably tried to find out who controls her.*

Nick licked his lips. "All I'm saying is that these bastards are feeding it to people. SYNTH. They're feeding it to people and nobody knows about it. There might only be Erewhon. There might only be this place. There might not be anything. Those bastards did it. They're laughing, too. Oh, they're laughing."

Detective Prior smiled, though there was no humor in it. "I leave all the thinking to guys like you, Nick. Good luck to you. Enjoy the book."

"They'll fucking take it away!" Nick tried to shoot up from his chair, was stopped by the chains. "What did you come here for? To gloat? To tell me some bullshit about Ole being dead? Ole's not dead! Ole can never die! None of us can."

Ever the words of a revolutionary. Or a terrorist.

★★★

Which books?

Books. Plural. But what's the point? There is no crime, but there is an investigation.

And the report. He needed to write a report. Why did Miles care so much about the report?

Am I the worst detective of all time? I do not know what I am investigating. It's just a jog through the past. The Potemkin Crew. I'm not going to look for Markus Olsen, am I? I should go home. Be with Anna.

Be with Anna. There was something.

He had already skipped the office. Did anyone care if he was not at work? Nobody had called his cellphone. Nobody tried to reach him.

Nick had suggested the city pumped SYNTH into the food, maybe into the water, and Dr. Sojo had hinted at the same thing. Revolutionaries love their conspiracies. What if they were right? What difference would it make? And what did that have to do with Irene? As soon as he'd tried to talk about his avatar, Dr. Sojo and Nick had SYNTH on their minds.

He went home, considered inquiring about dinner. Anna rarely made anything for dinner, as both of them preferred a combination of frozen dinners and some fruit once in a while. Their budget for food had always been tight.

Anna was already eating when he walked in. She was on the couch, spooning microwaved corn into her mouth. She was watching a gameshow on TV. Nick said hello, hung up his old jacket in the closet next to the new jacket that he had never worn, and opened the freezer to look for dinner.

"Have you paid the rent for this month?" Anna asked.

"Just need another week, I think," he said.

"We can't go on like this. We have to do something."

"Yeah."

"I'm not kidding, Jack. Both my avatars aren't getting jobs right now. I can't find work."

Prior found a box of French bread pizza in the freezer.

"I haven't been paid this week," Anna said. "And I did a huge job."

Prior wanted to ask what her actual job was on Erewhon. She used to help people customize avatars, and then when demand dried up, she began creating avatars for people, establishing entire lives and careers for people in the virtual world. She started doing other jobs on Erewhon, though he had failed to keep up with her. She didn't like to talk about work much, and neither did he. There wasn't much for him to talk about, anyway.

When Ole was still around, I always had something to say. The hacker's presence in his life had lent an element of danger and excitement. It was a high profile case. The Potemkin Crew was already a legend by the time he was assigned the job.

What would it be like to log on while using SYNTH? He had never done it. The virtual world had meant little to him while he was chasing Ole. The Potemkin Crew had been his obsession; the case had defined him, haunted him, kept him up at night. He tried to be Ole. What did the hacker eat? What did the hacker wear? Who did the hacker love? Poetry, it turned out. Fucking poetry.

Could he still get SYNTH if he wanted it? He had tried it once, maybe twice—he couldn't remember because he had certainly thought about doing it again, but was not sure how many times he actually visited with Dr. Sojo—and the world around him had become a rainbow of codes and processes that faded to black.

He waited until Anna went to bed and logged on to Erewhon. He stared at Irene in her virtual apartment. Chose an outfit. Checked phone messages. People were worried about her.

Irene might be dead, Prior thought.

And there would not be an investigation.

★★★

He wore the new jacket, the one he had never worn. Would people think he was Cash? A NoCred could never afford a jacket like this one. And it wasn't too late to sell it. He began to see the money handed to him by a benevolent hand. He counted the imaginary bills. It was almost like he already had the money.

"So where the hell were you yesterday?" Miles asked over the phone.

Detective Prior hated talking over the phone while driving. "Isn't it your job to know where I am at all times?"

"Anna didn't know where you were, either."

"You were at my apartment?"

"Listen, the chief asked about that report. I mean, I can do it myself. I try not to step on the shoes of a legend… "

"You're just lazy," Prior said. "You can write it yourself, like you said."

"I have something to finish up about our case, actually. I'm going over to the apartment, now."

"There isn't a case."

"Meet me at the dead guy's apartment." He hung up. Made the drive to the apartment where a man had died of a heart attack. *I would rather you just stayed in your hole*, he thought about his 'partner'. It was a vindictive thought, and he wasn't a vindictive man. What had Miles done to him?

Well, Miles had apparently visited his apartment yesterday, and Anna hadn't told him. *There is nothing between us. Nothing. There is nothing between me or anyone. There is only Irene. Before Irene, there was Ole. Before Ole, there might have been a man named Jack Prior.*

The detective drove off again to a different apartment.

★★★

Dr. Sojo had been waiting for him.

★★★

SYNTH asked the first question in technicolor, words bold, bright, somewhere.

Did Anna make Irene?

You mean, did Anna make the avatar?

That wasn't the question.

SYNTH used to ask a lot of questions. SYNTH is asking questions now.

★★★

Detective Prior drove through the blond city, past the downtown Cash towers, then a posh Cred neighborhood, then into the labyrinth of the NoCred sprawl, the everywhere. The everything.

He checked his cellphone. How long ago had Miles asked him to stop by the apartment where Carlo had died? Was that yesterday? Miles had not called again. He typed up a message to Anna about dinner, then changed his mind, didn't send it. There was an alert on his phone about the war. There was another update which implied Samarqand had extradited another writer and two poets, sending them to St. Petersburg.

The car was parked while he checked his phone.

SYNTH had an idea.

Detective Prior closed his eyes.

I'm listening.

Irene could help him with the investigation. She could investigate the manner in which Carlo had died.

You and Irene can go to Erewhon together.

SYNTH, I can't be Irene anymore. I don't know why.

You don't have to be her if she is you.

There was an application he could download to his phone. He had never done it because it cost money, and he preferred to work from home in the comfort and silence afforded by the presence of his wife sleeping in a room nearby. Besides, he was saving his money.

Amigo, why don't you realize there is no investigation? You want an excuse to chase Ole one more time.

SYNTH had a lot to say.

His new jacket looked like his old jacket. Was just as comfortable, was not stiff, did not smell new. This was the jacket he had chased Ole in. With his collar popped, hands in pockets. Put them there, now. Hands in the pockets. A real detective. Looking for a hacker-terrorist-poet in a city that had a fake version of itself, and people could go there. Live there.

There is more than one way to log on to Erewhon if you don't want to download the app for your phone.

★★★

Irene was tall, dark, and slender. She dated bad men who had money, bad men who womanized. Her longest relationship had been a matter of months because no man could keep up with her schedule. They wanted to see her, be seen with her.

The unreal version of Viborg City was crowded with unreal people controlled by real people. Irene said hello to people on the street who recognized her. She stopped into the coffee shop, checked her phone messages. How long had it been since she'd last worked a case?

I could be a soldier, instead, Irene thought. And she could. In Erewhon, you could be anyone, do anything. Some people actually chose to be NoCred in a virtual world in which you had to be either Cred or Cash just to have access.

It wasn't Irene thinking she could be a soldier. No, it was Prior. And Prior might have to throw Irene's career away to start a new avatar. Or maybe Irene could become a war hero? Wouldn't the press eat that up?

But Erewhon felt different, today. Erewhon felt more solid somehow, more substantial. As if he was not a man using a computer to be another person, but was a woman in a coffee shop who thought about a man named Detective Prior, or a man she imagined to exist.

Irene lingered in the coffee shop. Why would you want to serve coffee to people in a virtual world? You can be anyone, do anything. All you needed was money. Even in the unreal world.

There had to be cases she could take. Homicides to solve. Terrorists to pursue. It would be so easy to retract the South-East China attack on the Viborg City shopping center, the attack that had taken place just a couple years ago. She could prevent the attack. Make a difference in the war. And then South-East Chinese technology wouldn't be so expensive.

That wasn't true. Prices wouldn't change in the real world. *What am I doing here?*

The city's center was abuzz with traffic and light. A mockup of Times Square outside, only this was supposed to be Viborg City, only that wasn't true, either. And people watched. Identities were supposed to be secret, here. The only identity that mattered was the one you came with.

Irene stared into the coffee cup. There was no coffee in it. How long had it been empty?

She walked out the shop and wandered aimlessly. Stared at the virtual storefronts, was propositioned by prostitutes of all genders and no gender. The people behind these avatars were Cred and Cash.

Give me your money if you don't want it, Prior thought while Irene waved, smiled, said no thank you, pushed a man aside who touched her shoulder, kicked another man in the shin who tried to snatch her purse. She walked.

Was Erewhon always like this?

People did not openly attack her in Erewhon. Not usually.

I am a stranger here, he/she or she/he thought.

There were crimes to solve.

Irene hailed a cab, drove to the false version of the apartment where a man had died of a heart attack. There would be a virtual apartment, as Erewhon's builders did more and more to ensure the virtual world was a copy of the real one.

There should be an investigation. But this was not a thought that originated from anywhere. The cab driver may have said it. Irene may have said it. The words existed. *There should be an investigation.*

The cab arrived at the destination, and the virtual NoCred apartment was the same here as it was in the real world. An exact duplicate. She went in. There was no police tape in front of the door. There was no crime scene. *Because there wasn't a crime, not even in the real world. There is no investigation. But there is a report that must be written.*

She knocked. A short, bulky man answered the door. Dark circles beneath his eyes, he squinted at her. "Yes?"

"I'm Detective Irene Sanders. I'd like to ask you a few questions."

He nodded. "Yes. OK. That's fine."

"Don't bother inviting me in, Nick," she said. She removed her gun from the holster at her hip and shot him.

★★★

Detective Prior blinked, heard the pounding.

"Wake up, asshole," Miles said while he knocked on the window.

Prior rolled the window down.

"That's not my name," Prior said.

"Where have you been?"

"You asked me that before, and I said you're supposed to know. You're supposed to be watching me. Isn't that what they pay you for?"

"Out of the car, Prior."

Groggy, a dream escaping him, he stepped out. He instinctively wanted to check his gun, but he did not. He was parked outside the NoCred apartment where Carlo had lived. How did he get here? He didn't remember the drive.

I was on SYNTH, and I'm coming down. It doesn't have me. I haven't taken it in a long time. If I take it again... but I won't. I can't even say if it was a fun experience this time. I was... I was Irene again...

"All you were supposed to do was write the report," Miles said. "Let's take a walk."

Of course, Miles walked behind him. That's the way these sort of things are done. Detective Prior looked up at the sky and wondered if Ole would have written anything poetic about a colorless sky.

"So who is Carlo Bialer?" Prior asked as they walked up to the apartment. "You need an official report to say he was not murdered. He died of a heart attack. But he died another way. Can I assume you did it?"

Miles laughed.

"What difference does it make if I know?" Prior asked. "You needed me to do the paperwork, needed me to help clean up the rest of the old mess. What did you learn?"

"Give it a rest, Jack. Everyone works for Viborg City. Everyone who lives here works for the city, and will always work for the city. There's a war going on."

"Dodged my question."

"What is there to learn? I do what I'm told. Don't be angry with me. It's not personal."

"I'm not mad. You killed Carlo Bialer. He's connected to the Potemkin Crew somehow. That was your case, I assume. You were probably chasing Markus Olsen. Why did I have to get those books?"

"I don't know what you're talking about. Olsen? Nah. I worked for another department in the city. I was after Ole, except I got a chance to actually see the body."

Detective Prior swallowed. *Both of us, looking for Ole. We were looking for a poet, not a hacker. We were looking for a revolutionary.*

The yellow tape was still up in front of the apartment. He stepped over, and walked into the dusty old room. There was no reason for him to be here. There was no investigation.

"Which books?"

"Huh?"

Prior moved first. Pulled his gun. Fired into his partner's stomach. Miles had drawn his piece, was falling backward, clutching his stomach. It took forever for him to fall, his mouth twisting into an oval, his eyes widening with shock. Miles's gun was still in his hand, but it was slowly, slowly, dropping from fingers that had opened, lost their ability to hold the weapon, because this man was not a trained soldier, had been shot, his attention diverted by the sudden pain, the sudden shock that his life might not be anymore, all in a realization, all in a slow-motion moment, all now.

The detective had never killed a man, had never fired his gun at anyone.

He stepped over Miles, who groaned and begged for something. Prior didn't quite hear him. He was thinking about the doors that he heard opening in the hallway. People had heard the gunshot. And he should say something to Miles, some final line, but he was not a vindictive man. There was no reason to say anything.

Detective Prior stepped over the tape, saw all the doors in the hallway were closed. He looked behind him; Miles could still shoot at him. But Miles was not even on the ground. The room was dark.

Prior quickly walked out of the apartment building.

★★★

He was behind the wheel of his car again. The moment with Miles had been an interruption, an interlude.

Any minute now, the cops will be here.

I shot Miles. Irene has shot people. Maybe that is why I feel nothing.

The sky was not colorless. The sky was bright blue, too bright. Only a moment ago the sky had seemingly not existed at all.

He took out his cellphone, sent a message to Anna that was

an apology, changed his mind, didn't send it. Would she leave Viborg City with him? Would she be okay living the life of a NoCred? Maybe they could go to Samarqand, see the things that Ole had seen.

I had a dream, too. I had a dream that I was Irene. I had a dream that I found Nick's avatar and shot him. I know Nick is there, in Erewhon. They use him. He didn't deny it. But maybe he's not there anymore. Or, his avatar isn't.

In his dream, Nick's avatar lived in an apartment that was supposed to be Carlo Bialer's apartment. Why did Irene shoot Nick?

SYNTH had reminded him that he could use his phone to download the software to check into Erewhon from wherever he was. Erewhon on the go. A mobile world. Did he download it? He didn't have the money. He couldn't have downloaded it. Shooting Nick with Irene had been a dream. No use checking to see if he downloaded the app. What would that prove?

Besides, he could not be Irene anymore. He did not understand her. She was a stranger to him.

Prior sighed. He placed his gun on the seat next to him.

There would be no investigation.

Is that you, SYNTH? Have you always been here, with me?

Ole, the poet, had died in Samarqand.

There was still a way to find him, and Jack would be wearing his new jacket.

The Hard Game

Andrew Coulthard

Everything changes over the years, not least ourselves. I've heard people say that they haven't, that they are just the same as they were when young, but I think they simply don't remember.

Nothing remains the same.

As a kid, I loved games. I played board games with my parents and sisters, I played in the garden and street with my pals. As a teenager, it was all wargames and roleplaying; little figurines made of white metal or plastic. And in the end, when the prices fell, I went over to gaming on the computer.

My old dad bought the family's first computer; a Sinclair Spectrum. Cool. But we weren't allowed to play on it in case it got broken or the keyboard wore out. I hung out with my pal, Jim, instead and for the most part watched while he and his better mate Johnny explored the Elite universe on the Commodore 64. Sometimes I even got to play for a little while myself.

Games like those lived on magnetic tape cassettes and had to be reinstalled every time you wanted to play. I still recall the weird symphony of squeaks, squeals and chirps they made as we tried to load them into RAM. Sounded a bit like those fax-machines every workplace used to have. Hard to believe now…

In those days, games were both an end in themselves and something that I sensed would actually lead me somewhere; they formed a vital part of my life. But now that I'm old and I know life's a dead end, I've very little time for them…

I wake in darkness from a dream that's still vivid. But the colours and images soon begin to pale leaving only strange and beautiful feelings in their wake. Like life, even they fade before long.

The clock ticks loudly; an old, chunky, wooden block with an ivory face that has to be wound up with a brass key. It once belonged to my wife's grandmother and is still the best we have. All our more modern timepieces are unusable these days; you can't get the batteries any more, or rather you can, but they cost.

I roll over and wrinkle my nose. The blankets don't smell too good. We have a tub of Cleanobact: a sort of grey, coarse-grained paste crawling with artificial bacteria. It's effective against all kinds of dirt and we could use it to clean up with, but like everything else it's expensive. So, we have to reserve it for the kitchen and toilet bucket to keep them free of the multi-resistant bugs you get everywhere these days.

Anyway, there's soap. The Brothers down in Tanto make their own. It doesn't smell bad and works on most things. Cheaper too.

We've got purified, running water and, in this district, it's included in the rent. The amount we get is rationed to a few litres a day, which we mostly drink. If you want more you've got to pay. As for doing our business, we use a chem-bucket and the shared toilet drain in the cellar. We only wash our clothes now and then. It's cheapest to let The Brothers take care of that and whenever there's any money left over, that's what we do.

Sleep evades me. It's still pitch dark without the slightest hint of dawn and the lad's breathing fills the void. I've a dozen aches and pains, not least from my knees and ankles. I try for sleep again, but it's no good, I'm wide awake. This often happens now that I'm old. I want to sleep, not in order to rest and awaken refreshed, just to avoid the waking world and its discomforts. But sleep betrays me time and again selling me short as a torrent of thoughts, memories and feelings tumble through me.

An image surfaces in the murk. It's my wife as she was when she was young; so lovely. We met in England during the final years of the Cold War, not that anybody remembers that any more, or at least not those who've only been to *Pauper School*.

Pauper School is the colloquial name for our state run educational institutes. The primary education they offer is so limited it doesn't get you anywhere in today's world. If you want to do well in life you need to purchase supplementary educational modules. They're mostly delivered via hyper-media and if you have the right implants you can have the knowledge channelled straight into your head. But it all costs.

I see her face again, this time it's when she lay dying right here on this very bed sofa. Cancer. She was so pale and fragile near the end. When I was little they thought that cancer would be eradicated eventually, and it has been in a way. Just not for everyone.

The public hospitals couldn't afford the treatments her particular illness needed and we certainly couldn't stretch to private health care. So, she went the same way as her parents before her and mine too, come to think of it. I just hope my daughter gets a better life because I doubt my son will ever be able to afford medi-tec.

My thoughts wander back to my younger self. I was quite artistic once. The thought makes me laugh now. I used to draw and write poetry in my spare time. It seemed important back then and served as a counterpoint to all that gaming. So much changes over the years.

For a long time, I was convinced that I'd eventually be "*successful*", that everything would "*work out*". Although I never knew exactly how... illusions. Even when things have gone well nothing good has lasted.

During my early years, the world seemed one of extremes and the futures I imagined would either be of darkness or light: human life struck me as possessing such incredible potential, yet at the same time my friends and I were convinced we were going to be obliterated by nuclear war. That didn't happen. Instead I became acquainted with life's obstacles and gatekeepers and the endless reasons why I couldn't do this thing or follow that path. My peers and I started learning about the threat from our poisoned environment and climate change and the fragility of the economy. Oh yes, the danger of economic collapse was always present.

At the start of the 1990s I got married and moved from England to Stockholm in Sweden. A new start in a new land. The timing was pretty off, and we had to struggle through some really tough years of economic crisis. I learnt Swedish, did some dead-end jobs for lousy pay. I studied in my own time and, in the end, I got a more or less permanent position working in IT and education—businesses of the future, or so it was reckoned.

I became a dad and commenced what was probably the happiest and most meaningful chapter of my life. At the same time, that's when I first felt the creeping sensation that life was passing me by. Shit, I hadn't even begun realising my dreams, wasn't even sure what they were, yet suddenly mid-life was knocking at the door.

During the first decade of the 21st century there were ever greater changes. The world economy was totally buggered again. Before long the damage we'd been doing to the natural world really started to kick in...

I cackle out loud. In retrospect, my life sounds terrible, but there have been good times too. The extremes I envisioned as a kid turned out to be less dramatic in reality. Instead of black or white life's been a series of relatively minor dark-light oscillations. Whenever my situation got better it soon took a turn for the worse, as if the universe preferred grey to either end of the spectrum and was somehow always engaged in restoring order. Old Churchill once said something about that: what really counts isn't the successes or the failures but the courage to continue regardless of conditions. But I think my courage, such as it was, has run out.

I wish I could have done more for the lad, though. He's always been a good son and deserves a better life.

I yawn and feel myself drifting... The next time I wake up it's to a grey, rainy day. I sit up and sense how tired my body is. My joints are aching and there's a moment of anger. Medicines exist for that kind of thing, custom-bacteria and micro-machines that operate on you from the inside. And there are compounds that can be rubbed into your skin. The active ingredients sink through your dermis and rebuild the tissues beneath. Other smart-func agents can be injected directly into the joints to create new cells. You don't need a prescription, but as always, it's a question of money.

You can buy cheaper stuff on the black market of course, but there are risks. I've heard of people using smuggled goods and getting well, but even if you know the dealer, matters can go awry. There've even been a couple of cases on our block.

The old bloke who was our caretaker before the state took over was always a real lard-ball. He managed to wear out both his knees over the years, which caused him a lot of gip. So, he got himself a course of injections from a doctor with some bootleg medicines for sale. Trouble was the doc turned out to be a quacksalver of the worst kind.

We heard the old man's screams across the entire block for days. Then it went quiet. When they took him out his legs were so deformed they couldn't get his trousers on him. His entire lower body was a mass of purple and black swellings, legs like a bunch of grapes the size of footballs. There was something else growing between the grapes, looked like a gnarled tree root. They say he's still alive, but he's never been back here.

I shiver as I get dressed. Nowadays there's no heating other than what we can fix ourselves. We have the cooperative's solar panels on the roof and the lad and I have a few extra ones outside the window. We saved up and got them at a knock-down price from one of his mates—you can't beat contacts. But the electricity they produce has to be managed carefully. We need it for the computer and home-factory.

Even if it's a bit on the cold side, the flat's a good one. Built sometime near the end of the nineteenth century, it has high ceilings and bricked-up tiled stoves and the like. We were really lucky to be living here when the big changes began. It was a bit cramped when the kids were little and my wife was still alive, but for me and the lad it's pretty spacious.

Finally dressed, my bony feet move across the old floorboards. Broad, pale and gnarled, they flap down on thick leathery soles, causing tufts of dust to scatter around me. The laminate floor we had when I was young is long gone and I use bits of matting as stepping stones to reach the kitchen without getting splinters.

In the kitchen, I sink into my old Windsor chair and drink water from the bottle we always keep on the window ledge during the winter months. Our fridge is small, one of those ultra-low energy models that run on the clean-fuel briquettes they make in the Baltic States. We can't use the fridge for chilling water though. It's reserved for the few perishable goods we can afford, mainly organic Food-Source that we use in the *Lee Ho HF*, the home-factory we have for special meals and sometimes simple garments.

So, what's for breakfast today? Real food—the cooperative's own crisp bread, cheap and pretty good. We have a little oil left and beans of course. I mix the beans, oil and a pinch of synth-salt into a paste and spread it on the crisp bread, then I sit back down, chew slowly, my thoughts sliding back to the past.

All change: the kitchen is full of sound and sunlight. Everything is new. Was I ever really that young, energetic and strong? My daughter's laughter is music. In the bathroom, my son is singing his favourite hard rock tracks in the shower. On the cooker, bacon sizzles, the kettle is building up to the boil.

Sometimes there'd be sausage, black pudding or eggs; fruit juice or chocolate milk to drink, going over to tea and coffee as the kids got older. Always *real* food... God, we lived like kings.

Cold, silence, and increasing grey light from outside welcomes me back to the present. I get up and leave the kitchen, switching on the Low-En lamps in the hall and bathroom. The light they produce is rather sterile, but they use virtually no electricity. I'd love to splash out and get better lamps, or at least some coloured filters. Good lighting can do wonders. Maybe I'll be able to save up for some next year.

I go into the bathroom and use the bucket. It's not an ordinary one like you'd have had in the old days. This is a specially designed bucket-loo; an African model that works really well. Only half-full today, which means I can carry it down to the cellar. Good. Otherwise the lad would have to fix it. He doesn't complain, but I don't want to be a burden.

Before going I look in on him. Still asleep. I can't recall what he said he's doing today, but I don't think I was supposed to wake him. He came home late last night. He'd been out fishing again with his mates. Ussi, down in the park, mashes the fish and mixes it with potatoes and breadcrumbs to make spicy fishcakes to sell in Edin's Bar at Zinken's Crossing. They're supposed to be tasty, but I'd never eat them myself. Too many pollutants and whatnot. They always sell though and the lad gets good money from Ussi for the fish. Much needed. We use the money to buy food we *can* eat.

Curiosity leads me back to the hall. The chill-box is by the door. It's humming softly and the green panel leds are activated. Seems the lad was successful last night. I test the box's weight and can hardly lift it. A good catch.

The next step in the morning ritual is to connect the tablet and roll out the key-mat. Very old model, but once upon a time we could afford quality goods, so thankfully it still works. I check the account for messages, ever optimistic, though I should know better by now. There's nothing of course. Apart from the cooperative's info-transmission and the garden work-roster we haven't had anything for ages.

I log into Visnet. No messages there either. I'm always hoping my daughter will get in touch, but I don't have access to the networks that she's likely to be active on and nobody under sixty uses Visnet nowadays. It's been years since I last chatted with her. Back then she was in South America, planning to get married.

Time to get moving. I squint out through the kitchen window. It's above freezing out there, as usual. Here in Stockholm, it's been years since we had any snow that stayed more than an hour or two. You get frosty nights sometimes and the odd wet snow shower, but nothing more than that. I don't miss the cold, but the damp is hellish and causes aches in all my joints.

It's my turn to check with the coop-guard today. After that I'm heading south to Skarren, the market in Skärholmen, where the big furniture store once stood. It's the lad's birthday tomorrow and I'm hoping to get a few things for him. We've got some items to sell too. He found some tech-salvage last week, nice stuff, you know, rare metals etc. You can always sell that sort of thing at Skarren. He thinks that some of it is still useable; hope he's right, cause in that case we'll get what for us is really good money.

I'm not entirely sure where he gets it, but he often comes home with junk. I thought all the abandoned buildings had been picked clean and never find anything myself, but he and his mates are good at it. They've got better eyes I suppose.

I can see the coop-guard patrolling down there, but without my glasses I can't make out which one it is, the Russian I think. Hope so. He's a good sort. The residents' cooperative pays for security, us in other words. The guards are hired to protect our potato patches, although thieves are more interested in solar panels and bikes.

Memories well up again: when my son was little, the whole garden was covered in grass and bushes. There was a little play park, with swings and a slide, trees too. Every spring crocuses would bloom and then tulips. The kids used to play down there and in the summer, we'd all gather to barbecue meat with the other families... We had so much back then, didn't realise of course. Meat or fish every day, wine and beer too, if you wanted it. Sometimes on warm summer nights when the kids were in bed, my wife and I would sit out on the balcony. We'd talk about our plans for the future over tall drinks with ice. The balcony is covered in grow boxes now, but those vegetables are ours, not the coop's.

My flat is on the fourth floor and the stairs take time for an old man with tender joints and half-full bucket. I don't want to drop my burden or spill its cargo either! The bike and trailer are kept under lock and key down in the cellar. That's where the lad has hidden the junk as well. I empty the bucket into the drain, rinse it with Cleano-bact and place it beside the others. That's when I realise the flaw in my plan. The lad will have to come down and collect it when he gets up. Inconvenient for him, but I honestly can't face another trip up and down the stairs.

Next, a routine chat with the guard. The bulky figure is waiting by the potato patches, leaning on his night-stave. It is the Russian. He smiles when he sees me.

"How was your watch?"

"Rather wet, but otherwise fine," he says with a grin.

"Did you keep warm?"

"Sure. I have good clothes and the guardhouse is comfortable."

Security work pays well. Especially more risky assignments like this one. The guy is wearing self-cleaning garments and has an interactive tattoo on his face that shows he's trained, registered and possesses a valid licence. The smart-func ink has a secondary function, that of frightening potential combatants. If required, it can spread and change, covering his whole head and neck. Like all smart-func tattoos, the owner can also render it invisible if required.

His jacket changes colour over one shoulder only to go back to normal after a few seconds. I find myself staring at the material.

"Cleaning," he explains. "I program it to do this during nights when there's nobody about to look good for."

I nod. "Does it have other functions?"

He pulls up the hood. Suddenly, the whole jacket thickens, turning dark grey. The surface acquires a structure, like geometric scales. Next, the hood draws together across his face until only his eyes are visible. "Armour," he says, in a muffled voice. "Believe it or not, this thing is strong enough to stop a high velocity bullet. It'll even protect me from blast waves and shrapnel."

"A bullet. Not bad," I murmur, impressed.

The hood opens again and the material returns to its usual thickness and texture. "Expensive though," he replies with another grin.

"Of course," I agree.

Nice though it is, his jacket isn't the very best of its kind. The top brands look just like ordinary clothes, a sweater, jeans or a fancy suit, but they're strong enough to protect the wearer from just about anything. Ordinary people like us can't afford kit like that, however, not even guards.

"Did you see anything last night?" I continue.

He shakes his head.

"They came from that end of the garden last time, over the fence," I tell him, pointing to the furthest away perimeter.

"Yeah I know. But not last night. Those bastards keep well away when I'm here, rest assured."

Getting the bike and trailer up from the cellar is hard work. I cover the junk with an old sheet; don't want to encourage too much curiosity on my way to market. In the hallway, I pass through a steel gate that has acted as the entrance point to the building ever since the original outer doors were deemed too insecure. In the porch, I give the street outside the once over. There's no glass in the heavy bevelled wooden doors, hasn't been for years and I lean out, peering first one way then the other.

The sky is lighter and the rain has given way to drizzle. The street appears empty. To be on the safe side I wait.

Still nobody.

Getting to Skarren is not entirely without danger. On a good day, you can just ride your bike there and back again. But there are bad days when you need to choose your route with care. I have a wooden baton in a holder on my bike frame, which I can easily access if anyone tries anything.

I open the doors, mount my bike and ride out onto the pavement. This is often the most dangerous moment. You need to get going and away as fast as you can. I wobble a bit until I get my speed up, then I'm out in the centre of the street heading for Ringway and Horn's Street.

Some of Edin's men are stationed in the crossroad, keeping the peace. They have warm clothes, old motorbike helmets and quilted armour overcoats. Nothing fancy like the Russian's jacket. They know my son and recognise me. One of them says, "Hi," others wave and nod. I return their greetings and stop next to them.

"Where are you off to today?" their leader asks.

"Down to Skarren," I reply.

"Yeah? Which way are you going?"

"Liljeholmen and then the E20 or E4," I say, but he shakes his head.

"There's trouble in Liljeholmen. A lot of fighting last night in Aspudden and Midsommarkransen too."

"Really?" I reply, concerned.

"Fraid so. Better for you to take the long way. Ride down to Globen and then towards Älvsjö. Should be alright that way, I think."

I don't like this at all. There are a number of wooded areas adjoining that route and, as a rule, woods are even more dangerous than the city parks. The only park I trust at all is nearby Tanto and that's only because Ussi and The Brothers run things down there. As soon as you get over Årsta Bridge or past the old tolls at Skanstull, however, you're in danger again.

The Ringway is empty. I ride as fast as I can, keeping to the centre of the road. Down by Skanstull some men are loitering on the street corner at the crossing. I don't recognise them. They don't have armour, but some are carrying sticks. They glower at me as I ride by and turn uphill onto Skanstull Bridge towards Gullmars. I can't see anyone on the bridge. That's good.

Gullmars and Globen City are run by the Johannes Cooperative. They do a good job too. You have to pay to pass through, but it's not too expensive and you're safe as long as you're in their district. The adjacent districts however, including the once popular and upmarket Hammarby Harbour are nowhere near as healthy.

When I arrive at Gullmars on the far side of the bridge it's to find the barricades closed. I come to halt and a guard appears from inside the fortified guardhouse. She has good gear, full protection helmet and jacket armour as good as the Russian's. Better even.

"What's happening?" she asks.

"I'm on my way to Skärholmen," I reply.

"Really, going there? We have a market too, you know."

The guard is right, they do have a market in Globen City. But their cooperative is so successful, it pays taxes and gets benefits from the state. They even have their own ICT infrastructure for the residents. That means education, healthcare, info-services and business opportunities. All good. They make money via info-systems and trade with other, successful cooperatives.

The problem for outsiders like me is that their market is monitored by state inspectors who make sure trade is legal and the appropriate taxes are levied and paid. You can't trade in questionable goods, like junk.

"I have a meeting in Skärholmen with a good friend and that's why I need to go there," I lie.

She gives me a sideways glance for a moment. "Where are you from?"

"Southside. Close by. Zinken's Crossing..."

"Zinken? Well aren't you taking the long way to where you're going? Step closer please, I want to run an ident on you."

I scowl. I loathe idents; don't want people knowing where I go or what I do. It's an old attitude that I brought with me from my homeland. To be honest it's quite stupid, because somebody, somewhere always knows where you are and what you're doing.

She produces a small, black sphere with a hole on one side.

"Right thumb in here," she chirps, indicating the hole.

"Yes, yes, I know what to do," I mutter. "I've been in the game awhile... I'm over eighty for your information." I thrust my thumb into the sphere and the device starts reading my DNA.

"Yeah..." she murmurs. "You look older, actually."

She's really starting to piss me off. "Not everyone has access to the health products you do," I snap. At first I expect her to return my anger, but she's too busy scanning what the device is transmitting to the implants in her helmet and head.

"British..." she says.

"*Was.* I've been Swedish for decades, surely you can see that!"

"Yeees, I see that. Pensioner. State-owned accommodation. Former IT-teacher. Had your own firm for a long time. Wife deceased; daughter abroad, whereabouts unknown; son, long-term unemployed. You've no criminal history at least..."

"Thanks, I'm aware of that."

"But I can't be, can I?" she says, voice louder, patience starting to fray. "That's why we *have to* run checks sometimes."

I shrug and say nothing. Can't afford to push her too far.

"What's in the trailer?" she says, a sly note coming into her voice.

"Are you serious? What are you, an ex-cop or something? Look, I just want to pay the toll and pass through your district. I told you, I'm meeting my friend."

"Why choose this route?"

"Because the guards at Zinken said there's been trouble in Midsommarkransen," I explain.

She stays quiet for a while and I wonder what's happening behind her full-visage visor. Then she seems to make up her mind.

"Not just in Midsommarkransen, my friend. We have some restrictions in operation today. Wait here and I'll check with my Chief." She disappears behind the barricade.

I'm growing worried again. I've never known there to be a problem getting through the gates at Gullmars. While I wait, I ride my bike over to the edge of the bridge and gaze down at what was once *Hammarby Sea Town*. That's where the up-and-comings once aspired to live; a new city district with its own manmade ski slope.

The Baltic is a good bit higher than it was when the *Sea Town* was built, however, and it's become a *Sea* Town in ways never intended. Many of its apartment buildings are surrounded by water. Several other parts of Stockholm met the same fate and Old Town is ringed in by a concrete seawall.

When they learnt first-hand that all those dystopian climate prophecies weren't just the ramblings of crazy liberals and lefties, the residents emptied their cellars and moved out. First, their luxury apartments were reoccupied by homeless people; a big step up for them even with the power and water cut off. Later, however, gangs replaced the homeless, adapting the residencies and adding solar panelling and fuel efficient generators. The place hasn't been safe for ordinary citizens since. Worse still, there's a lot of forest beyond Hammarby and that always means danger.

The drizzle has stopped by the time the guard returns. I cycle back to the barricade.

"If you want to come in and enjoy the services our market offers, you're welcome. But we're not letting anyone through today."

"What? I don't get it. Are you saying your southern barricades are closed?"

"Correct. The Chief said the city police don't want anyone passing through this way because of last night's battles."

"Battles?"

"Yeah. We don't know if it was raids against civilians or all out gang war and the cops won't say. All we're sure of was that it was big."

"But how will I get to Skarren?"

"Don't know. Not through here."

I ride slowly back across the bridge and stop a while in the centre of the multi-lane expanse of concrete and asphalt. Along the horizon there are thin smoke trails over Liljeholmen. I squint and make out tiny black dots circling in the skies above the smoke. Drones.

I reckon I can forget about Skarren today. Hell's teeth. I wanted to get some new patterns for the factory and more Food-Source. The lad used to love Chicken Tikka Sizzler when he was a nipper and they had a pattern for it when I was last there. We need more yeast and a new wine kit too.

I decide to cycle down to the park and talk to the Bothers' people about the situation. They might be able to give me some suggestions or propose somewhere else I can buy and sell what I want.

When I get closer to the end of the bridge I put on a burst of speed, but the men who were there earlier are gone. After that I ride back along Ringway until I cross the railway and turn left onto Zinken's Way. There are guards all over the place along the road, but they let me pass. They're not well-equipped like the Russian or the guard at Gullmars. These are Ussi's and the Brothers' folk. They're much more like Edin's guards.

The allotments that once lined the road before have been extended now that affordable food is so important. They've swallowed the football pitches and cover the sports ground where I used to go skating with the kids. Even the park areas stretching from old Hotel Zinkensdamm down to the water are covered with a patchwork of cultivation plots.

Ussi holds court in the former hotel with his family and employees. Almost all the houses that once lined the park from the 60s, 70s and 80s are gone. The materials they were made of didn't last.

I greet the door guard, tell him about my situation and wonder if they know what's going on. The door opens and Ussi steps out. He's seen me through the loophole. He's as old as I am, but can afford good products so he looks more like a 40-year-old.

"Hello there, come on in a moment. There's coffee," he says smiling broadly.

In his office, we sit down in big, soft armchairs with huge cushions. The room smells good. There's a coffee table made of what looks like real wood. On it is a traditional style hardback book. All very impressive. He sees me looking at it.

"Poetry by Doubinsky," he says. "Do you know his work?"

I shake my head. "I used to like poetry, once," I say.

He has coffee and even biscuits. I'm so unused to sugar that I think the biscuits are too sweet and pretty disgusting, but the coffee is good. We small talk about life and he asks how things are for us.

"What can I say?" I begin with a shrug. "Things went the way they went. I've got to put up with old age and its discomforts. The worst thing I think is that I'm over 80 and still struggle to scrape together the rent."

"Are you behind with your rent?" he asks, troubled.

"Not really. I pay the rent with my pension. What costs most is food, at least if we want to eat stuff that doesn't make us sick."

Ussi nods. "Many don't have a pension at all. Some might say you're lucky."

"Yes, I know. I'm probably one of the very last who'll get a state pension at all. The glass is half-full in that respect. But you know, I only reached pension age a few months ago, and they'll only let me have this monthly pocket money for three years, max. Where will we get our rent money after that? My son's a useful lad, but life hasn't always been easy for him and I'm afraid I'll become a burden."

Ussi nods again. "You speak like a good father. You want to help your son and do right for yourself. I like that."

I shrug. "We do what we can."

"I like your lad too," Ussi continues. "He's straight in his dealings, trustworthy and not an idiot like some out there. Does he have fish for me today?"

I nod.

"Good. I'm going to help him and I'm going to help you too. You've got some goods to sell, this much I know. I think you need to talk to some of my friends at Skarren, okay?"

"Sure," I reply, surprised.

"Do you know the traders down there?" Ussi asks.

"Some... the ones dealing in Food-Source, wine kits and the like," I explain.

"No, no, don't bother with them. Talk to Moses, the tall, dark-skinned guy in Side-Hall B. I'm going to let him know you're coming. He'll help you, offer you good prices. He's got some nice stuff to sell too."

"Thanks," I say, genuinely pleased.

"You're welcome. I want your boy to have a good birthday..."

"You know about that?" I ask, surprised.

"I like to stay informed about people. Especially those with... potential. Now, there have been a few problems, so my employees will escort you to Älvsjö. After that, you should be fine."

I understand that our meeting is at an end and get up. "Thanks for the coffee," I say and Ussi nods. Then he takes out a gold neck chain with a locket from beneath his shirt. He opens the locket and mumbles something I can't hear. An image of a very tall man appears on one wall of the office.

"Hi Moses, how's life?" Ussi says with a smile.

I leave him.

Outside, a group of guards is waiting a few metres distant. I wait. After a couple of minutes have passed, one of them, a young woman with dark eyes and facial tattoos of the non-smart type, puts a hand to her left ear. She glances at me, nods and then summons the group and they move toward me.

"I'm Dilek. We are going to accompany you to Älvsjö," she announces. "Ready?"

I take hold of the handlebars and saddle of my bike and they surround me like a guard of honour. Then we set off, walking further into the park and up the access ramp to New Årsta Bridge.

The bridge is a massive, reinforced red concrete rail viaduct, with accompanying foot and cycle paths. It runs parallel to an older bridge from even earlier in the last century. Both have aged well. In my younger days, I used to go jogging here, across the viaduct and along the waterside path on the opposite, wooded shore of Årsta bay. Would never think of doing that now, not even if my knees allowed it.

There used to be a lot of rail traffic here once, especially commuter trains. But since Stockholm's population migrated to various autonomous smart districts, that kind of public transport isn't needed any more.

Modern trains are different, completely without traditional propulsion methods like diesel for example. Instead there are hybrid solutions combining gas turbines and organic so-called hyper-batteries. They charge themselves and provide the trains with near zero-polluting power. Today in Sweden, most rail traffic is goods related.

Abroad, there are the international maglev and vacuum driven tunnel-train systems. The Trans-Atlantia, Trans-America, Trans-Asia and Trans-Africa lines are the biggest, but there are others.

Mind you, Swedes have always loved their roads. Nowadays they're used by driverless electric cars with hyper-batteries or the newer thorium fuel cells.

I have my bike.

As we approach the far side of the bridge, the guards grow quiet. We are now beyond Tanto's limits and thereby beyond the Brothers' and Ussi's protection. We continue along Årsta Forest Way. The quickest path from here would be to turn up towards the E4, but that's exactly what we can't do today. Instead they're going to escort me along the railway toward Älvsjö and from there I must make it alone.

The tattooed woman stops suddenly. She signals to the others to get out of sight and then lies down at the side of the road. Puzzled, I wheel my bike off the road and crawl over to her.

"What is it?"

"Shut up!" she says and points to a ten-metre high rocky outcrop running parallel with the far side of the multi-track railway.

At first, I can't see anything. Then it seems as if something isn't quite right at a point near the top of the rock. I rub my eyes, but the odd visual effect remains. An area roughly two metres square is blurred, almost like a heat haze. And it's moving along the ridge. Above the haze, a little bird hovers and darts in a fashion that doesn't look entirely natural.

"What the hell is it?" I whisper.

The guard shakes her head then leans close. "Must be police, or maybe even a soldier. That bird is obviously a drone, but the blur effect... *really* nice kit. My guess is we're looking at some sort of invisibility surface, perhaps on a battle-suit."

The heat haze has stopped moving.

"He can see and hear us. No point in lying here," she continues. "Okay everyone, up you get. On your feet. No stupid moves."

We all stand up and remain still, awaiting the haze's next move. But after a couple of minutes it vanishes without a trace as does the bird.

"Alright," the guard leader sighs, her relief obvious. "Let's continue."

We don't get more than twenty metres before a grey two-metre metal tube glides out of the trees on our right where it has been waiting. It's one of the city's security drones and flies on short, broad wings equipped with rotors. Streamlined metal boxes beneath the wings house weapon systems.

The drone turns towards us, hovering at a height of roughly three metres and comes to halt a couple of metres in front of us.

"Remain still for ident." The voice is a recording. The eye positioned in the drone's snout flickers and changes colour several times.

"Guard Commander Dilek Andersson, registered and licensed. Permit valid until..." and the drone proceeds to list everyone's name and registration details, all except mine.

"One of your company lacks a transmitter or readable badge. Kindly provide an ident for this individual, Dilek Andersson."

"We're escorting him to Älvsjö. There was trouble last night," Dilek explains.

"Is he a prisoner?"

"No, he's just a citizen who..."

"Come closer, citizen."

With a sigh, I leave my bike and walk slowly toward the drone. I've been through this type of security check before. There's really nothing to worry about, but I've never been comfortable around these machines and my pulse starts to rise the closer I get.

The drone dips its snout so that it is directly before my face.

"Look directly into the scanner. Do not blink."

I do as I'm told.

"You seem very keen to get to Skarren today. Don't you know these districts are currently unsafe?" The machine voice has been replaced by that of an operator stationed in one of the city's distant control rooms. At first, I'm so taken aback by the switch that I'm lost for words.

"I see from your retinal ident that you're British. Do you speak Swedish sir?" the operator continues in perfect English. "Our systems have you travelling to Gullmars this morning on your way to the market in Skärholmen..."

Always the same story! "I was British, years ago," I fume. "I've spoken perfect Swedish for a very long time. You didn't give me a chance to reply, that's all. I'm meeting an important contact and he's only here for today. That's why I must get there, despite the situation."

"And you can't conduct your meeting over a comm-link?"

"I don't have a comm-link," I mutter.

"According to our information you are connected to the State Base Channels: email, televideo, Visnet etc. Wouldn't one of those do?"

"Oh yeah, them. Sure, I'm connected to those. I meant I don't own a handset or smart-func-garment, you know, that connects you to the whole world and all that crap."

"So? Why won't these channels suffice?"

I do my best to keep my temper in check. "You'll have to excuse me if I seem old fashioned, but sometimes it's nice to develop a nuanced connection with your acquaintances. You know, communicate *face-to-face*. Be present physically."

"Ah, are we talking about a romantic connection?"

I stare into the camera for a moment. "I'm over eighty years old. Do I look like I'm in love?"

"Then we're talking about a business contact. You are registered as a pensioner. A company was once connected to your citizen's registration details, but was deactivated some time ago. How are you handling the taxation on your business transactions?"

"Please, when I talk about my contact, I mean... it's not business... or sort of, maybe. Our discussions are at the planning stage. Today's meeting might lead to some sort of deal in time, I don't know."

"Thank you and good luck with your meeting. You will be contacted by the State Central Taxation Council at the end of this quarter for a tax audit. What's in the trailer?"

I become nervous, not because junk is illegal per se, but environmental regulations are very strict these days. I may have broken a whole range of them without realising. As if that's not enough, there are other risks. If the things my boy has found in actual fact belong to somebody else, I'm going to be in serious hot water. Not that the lad would consciously steal, but professional thieves sometimes hide their hauls in the ruins. He might have stumbled on stolen goods by mistake.

I move with wooden steps toward the trailer. The drone follows me. The members of my escort detect my nervousness and step back or to one side. I feel like a doomed convict on his way to the gallows, my executioner looking over my shoulder.

A distant boom is followed by the rapid crackle of small arms fire. After a split second's silence the machine voice returns.

"Thank you for your cooperation, citizen." Rotors buzzing, the drone ascends several metres into the air and accelerates away over the trees. Seconds later a dark pillar of smoke twists up above the treetops. It can't be more than a couple of kilometres away.

Dilek approaches me. "I don't know what you're planning to sell at Skarren, and I'm not accusing you of anything, but that felt a bit too close for comfort."

I sigh and nod.

"How about we get you to the drop off point as fast as possible?" Dilek suggests.

They leave me in Älvsjö, which is eerily derelict. I don't hang out here often, but there are usually stalls selling various home-grown or baked victuals, cyclists like me and plenty of pedestrians. Today there isn't a soul. So, I keep to the centre of the roads and cycle for all I'm worth towards Skarren.

After what feels like a long time, I glimpse the market's distinctive silhouette rising against the grey-black sky. You can't mistake its unique form, which has both crumbled in places over the years and been added to. I grin and a burst of energy allows me to increase speed. Despite everything, today's mission might just get accomplished.

The company that originally built Skarren only has outlets in the world's biggest cities these days. Stockholm and its satellites are too small. Their Nordic subsidiary operates a Swedish terminal up north somewhere and those living in Smart Districts can order patterns for furniture and fittings via their communication systems. The goods are then produced locally in the District's shared production facilities. Preconstructed furniture is still delivered on scheduled delivery days, but it doesn't happen often and the numbers of items are few. The price tag for those who want pre-constructed products and special deliveries is prohibitive.

As I draw closer to my destination the streets are full of people providing a stark contrast to the abandoned quarters I've been travelling through. I cycle by street market stalls and guard posts without being called over, arriving at last at the grand entrance. There I dismount and walk my bike through the huge doors. The enormous main hall, is teeming with folk.

An official dressed in Skarren's tunic and trousers approaches. No smart-func materials as far as I can see, just leather-like textiles in the market colours with *Skarren* printed across the chest in black.

"Buy or sell?" the man intones.

"Both," I reply.

"Who are you? What district?"

"From Högalid Cooperative," I reply.

His forehead furrows and he seems distant for a moment. I'm guessing that he's consulting some internal database or other.

"Oh yeah, okay," he says when he's done. "The main hall is right ahead here."

"But I'm meeting Moses," I object. "I think he's in Side-Hall B."

The official looks sceptical. "You're meeting Moses Oscarsson?"

"Yes, I've just come from Ussi in Tanto."

"Alright, but I don't recognise you. Do you have a badge or some other token from Ussi?"

I shake my head.

"If you're one of his employees, we can do an ident. That'll give me your contract number."

"That won't help," I admit. "I'm not an employee. My son helps him now and then. I was with Ussi an hour ago, in his office. We drank coffee."

The official stares at me briefly then his features settle into a scowl. "Drank coffee, did you? Listen old man, if you don't show me who you are, you're not meeting Moses; I don't trust you. In fact, forget it. You're not getting in here at all today. Go on, clear off."

I'm about to leave, when a giant of a man strides towards us through the crowds. He is heavily built, broad in the shoulder and his shaved head is covered in tattoos and skin ornaments. The inked images are in constant motion and I suspect that at least some of the ornaments are the visible end of comms implants or some other form of smart-func device.

"He's expected," the giant rumbles and the official turns away, busying himself with something else. Satisfied, the giant turns to me: "How's it going? I work for Moses. Follow me."

"How did you know who I was?" I ask.

The giant gives a snort. "Let's just say we had our sights on you before you even entered the building."

He cleaves through the crowd like one of those

icebreakers that used to operate in the northern Baltic once upon a time. I struggle to keep up, wheeling my bike through broad galleries and corridors. Each space is thronged with people engaged in trade and exchange, but they all step aside to let us pass.

At last we come to a very large room, high-ceilinged with concrete walls and floor. The room has been divided up into booths and stands. There are lots of people here too, though not as many as in the other spaces we've passed though.

Merchants and buyers regard me with undisguised suspicion as we walk by, making me very uncomfortable.

We arrive at a high doorway and the giant tells me to wait outside, before going through the door. I lean my bike against the wall and sit down to wait. The market folk continue to stare and I fix my gaze on my feet.

"What've you done?" a trader calls from behind his stall. "Is Moses pissed off with you?"

"I haven't done anything," I say.

One of the customers comes over to stand before me. He has good quality clothes, probably made from smart-func materials. He's also wearing a weird headdress, which reminds me of an Egyptian pyramid with a broad fur border around the base. His face is thin, the features angular. I can't see his eyes because he's wearing white, protective lenses that cover the visible surfaces.

"What have you here?" he asks, pointing at the trailer.

"Nothing that concerns you," I reply trying to sound more confident than I feel.

"Who the hell are you to decide what concerns me?" he snarls and takes hold of the covering cloth. I just have time to struggle to my feet when the door opens behind me and the giant reappears.

The man with the protective lenses lets go of the cover and backs away to disappear into the crowd.

"What was he doing?" the giant asks.

"He wanted to check out the goods," I reply.

"Didn't you warn him off?"

"Yes, but he only got angry and did it anyway."

"Angry?" The tattoos writhe across the big man's head and his thick features contract into a furious scowl. He strides over to the merchants. "Who was that? Come on, somebody has to know."

But the marketeers and their clientele shake their heads and look away or down at their feet.

"Alright then, we'll check surveillance," the giant continues. "We're going to find that bastard and if it turns out that he's connected to any of you..." He leaves the sentence unfinished.

The giant helps me unload the junk. I ask him if I can take the bike when we go in, but he just laughs.

"Listen grandad, nobody's going to touch your bike, believe me." I'm not so sure but don't dare say so.

On the other side of the door there's a little room with two other exits.

"You go through that door," he says pointing to the one on the right. "We don't like product-DNA, body-cookies and the like round here. There are devices in the walls through there that'll neutralise all that stuff. The goods will be treated separately. I'll take care of them, okay?"

I nod and he disappears with the junk through the left-hand door. The next room is even smaller than the first. It's unfurnished, the floor is bare concrete and it's pretty dark.

"Just stand still a moment." The giant's voice is coming through a hidden speaker somewhere. I do as I'm told. After a few seconds, it grows lighter and a door appears before me in what had appeared to be a bare wall. It opens on a luxurious chamber, even more impressive than Ussi's headquarters, with rugs, wall hangings and large, soft furniture.

Most likely everything in here is smart-func one way or another. The walls are probably constructed to block the authorities' and competitors' probes; a painting or cushion might monitor and record everything that takes place: images, sound, temperature, humidity, the lot. There are doubtless various defence tools here too.

The items I brought are mainly different components. The giant arranges them on a table in the centre of the room and I sit down on a very comfortable chair beside it. Some pieces are quite old. I can expect a little money or maybe some goods for them. But several look like they might be more modern while a few I don't recognise at all, including two blue cylinders with no markings, ports or controls. They might not even be technology and if so, won't be worth much, if anything.

I hear the giant's voice: "Yes, right outside. He was about to rummage through the old man's bike trailer when I arrived. The bloody nerve. Some people just don't have any respect."

"Could it have been one of Mirsad's employees?"

"I don't know... no, surely not."

"Cop?"

"Would a cop go on like that?"

"Alright. Find out who it was if you can. Let's be extra vigilant for a while."

A very tall, slim man with dark skin comes into the room. I recognise him as the one who appeared on Ussi's wall. He pauses a moment to give me the once over. Unsure how to respond, I remain sitting and don't meet his gaze. Moses is dressed in a classic cut old-fashioned suit, white shirt and tie. He's wearing sunglasses.

The glasses are smart-func and are reading me while he watches. Sometimes kit like that is connected to external databases. They can be used to carry out idents based on someone's appearance. Police and guards occasionally have them. The really cool ones can scan your body chemistry and facial micro-expressions, or your hand movements to detect when you might be lying.

"Good afternoon, I'm Moses Oscarsson. Welcome to my offices." It seems he's done scanning. The chair is low, which isn't good for my knees. I get up with a grunt, and take the large hand he's extended.

"My business partner, Ussi Magnusson, has told me you're a friend of his and that you would like to sell some items. Is that right?"

"Yes, although I'd most like to trade my goods for others. Don't trust currencies that much."

"Not even our local micro-currency," Moses says. "It's very hard to trace, you know."

"Mmm, yes it's okay, but I'd still rather trade."

"Well that's fine. Let's see what you have here..." He sifts through the junk, with a theatrical air, picking up the odd piece to examine it thoroughly. "Hmm, okay..."

But his interest is feigned, perhaps for the sake of being polite. He leaves the old stuff and moves on to the newer pieces. From his demeanour, I realise they're nothing special either. Disappointing.

When he spots the blue cylinders, however, he pauses and his affected air vanishes. He picks up one of the cylinders. His eyes narrow and his lips part slightly. He glances at me and then back at the cylinder and appears lost in thought. I start to feel nervous.

"And you cycled all the way here from Zinken's Crossing with these?" he says at length.

I nod and swallow, my throat dry. "Is it just crap?" I ask.

"Crap?" He smiles but remains quiet for a few moments, then seems to reach a decision. "I promised my friend Ussi that I'd give you a good price for your goods and I shall. What would you like?"

"Well, we need some items back home: a wine kit, yeast, Food-Source for the household factory. And then, I'm hoping to be able to get a new pattern for the factory. It's my son's birthday tomorrow. Long ago we used to go to that Indian restaurant that was on Horn's Street. He loved Chicken Tikka Sizzler and last time I was here I saw..."

"Chicken Tikka Sizzler?" Moses interrupts me with a burst of laughter.

"Yes," I reply, nervous again.

"Old man, you shall have it. *Kalle!*"

"Yep," the giant shouts from the next room.

"Get the bankcard, go and buy some things for our guest, here. We'll make you a list. And you, old feller, the wine kit and Chicken Tikka are a present for your boy. I'll pay you both with something else."

Pleased, but puzzled I sit down with Moses. The cylinders are apparently worth something, but I still don't know what they are. On reflection, maybe that's for the best. We drink coffee and Moses asks about our home situation, what my son does with his time, and how much he works for Ussi. He gives me a pendant for my son. I know what it is, it's a comm device, like the one Ussi used when I was there. I don't really understand what's happening, but I thank him anyway and put the device in my pocket.

"I want your boy to contact me," Moses continues. "Ussi told me he's reliable and if that's the case I don't think he should waste his time on fishing and the like. He can work for us instead. I'm talking proper wages and benefits."

Twenty minutes later I'm standing outside while several assistants load my trailer. Moses has given me a whole bucket of Food-Source, a catering pack like the ones restaurant's use. The container is self-refrigerating, so I don't need to worry about getting it into our little fridge. It'll provide over a hundred meals for me and the lad. He's also fixed me factory patterns for Chicken Tikka Sizzler, Lamb Vindaloo, Naan, Merlot and Chardonnay. And that's not all. There's a traditional wine kit *and* yeast. We use wine kits because they're cheaper than wine patterns for the factory, but now we've two of those as well!

"Right that's the birthday presents. Time for your payment," Moses says and claps me on the shoulder.

I can't quite believe what's happening. His men load a large tub of Thing-Source, the base substance from which our factory can produce tools, clothes and what have you. It's expensive and we haven't had any for years. Unfortunately, we don't have any patterns for clothes or tools, but Moses has thought of that too.

"This a pattern for a jacket for your boy. When somebody works for me, I want them to dress right for the job."

The pattern is foreign, from China. I read the Swedish description on the pattern packaging:

Smart-func jacket with autodynamic temperature control suitable for a range of different climate zones. Includes: full infrared shielding function, patented background-blend mirroring, multiple camouflage technology and full protection against low energy projectiles.

I am speechless. And that's still not everything. Moses hands me a quadratic ceramic box.

"This is a heater. It uses energy briquettes, the standard sort. It'll warm up your entire flat in an hour and not only that, a single briquette will keep it going at full effect for about twenty-five hours."

I shake my head. *We're rich!* "What *were* those cylinders?" I stutter.

"Your son might know. If he finds any more, he should let me know with the pendant. I'll send Kalle to come and collect them, okay?"

I nod. "Thanks, Moses."

Kalle accompanies me to the exit where he spends a few moments speaking to the staff. From now on, I'm always to be admitted without questions. The staff nod and I am photoed and registered in their equipment. After that I leave.

Directly outside there's a stall selling mussels and shrimp. I'm sorely tempted to splash out, but the prices are very low and I haven't forgotten what happened after our cooperative garden party last summer. A couple living opposite staged a little pre-party reception for some friends from another cooperative. They bought a consignment of cheap mussels and produced copious amounts of bubbly with their household factory. The day after, everyone who'd eaten the mussels was sick. Then, a few days on, a couple of the guests died and the hostess's hair turned greenish and fell out. She's still bald. I decide not to bother.

Then I notice somebody watching me from the crowded street. It's the guy with the pyramid hat and protective lenses. I'm not afraid of him now I've become friends with Moses, but it's probably time for me to get going.

I leave the crowds behind and ride through the desolate streets of Älvsjö without meeting a single person. It's late afternoon, but I'm not worried. Instead I'm almost giddy with happiness. I feel strong, invincible. This morning I'd hoped I might be able to trade some technical scrap for a food pattern and a small amount of Food-Source. The wine kit and yeast

I was expecting to have to buy with my bank tag. But now... bloody hell, the lad and I really are rich!

It's almost dark by the time I get onto Årsta Forest Way and I ride like a maniac to reach New Årsta Bridge and the safety of Tanto.

I notice something strange ahead. It appears from nowhere, like a patch of heat haze and shadows. It looks like the soldier we saw earlier. But I'm riding full tilt and don't intend to stop for anyone or anything.

A voice issues from the heart of the haze: "Look out!" A tiny bird swoops down toward me and there's a shout from behind. Next thing I know, I'm spinning through air and then everything goes dark.

★★★

My head is throbbing, pressure mounting behind my eyes. My body hurts too. Everywhere. An angel appears before me. She's so lovely. Beautiful face. Perfect skin and teeth. But her body is incorporeal, like lines and patterns of pure light and darkness. She could be made of water.

She's doing something to me. Her heat haze hands are touching my head, my body and legs. I reach out, wanting to touch her, connect with the mirage.

"Keep still, I'm almost done."

"What are you?" I ask, confused.

"What am I? I'm your rescuer."

"But your body..."

"My body? Oh, that's my clothes." Suddenly she becomes fully visible and I realise she's an ordinary young woman. What a disappointment.

"What happened?"

"You were attacked. They were waiting in the trees to rob you."

Then, with a growing sense of dread, I recall the bike and my goods. I sit up and pain explodes all over my body.

"No, keep still! The analgesics will kick in in a couple of minutes. The rest will be effective in about quarter of an hour. You can move around then."

"But my stuff," I complain.

"Yeah, you've still got a few things," she says. She has a rucksack full of equipment and a very impressive mini-field hospital kit.

I continue to object. "Isn't it dangerous staying here?"

"They won't be back. Two of them are up there on the slope. My drone took them with its micro-darts. They won't come round for three or four hours. If the others do return, my little birdie here will sort them out in short order."

"Bird? It was you we saw across the railway earlier."

She nods.

"Are you with the military?"

"No, I'm a student."

"*Student?* With kit like this? Good grief, when I was young, students lived below the bread-line. Just look at all these medicines, and the bird alone must have cost half a million."

"Actually, I built it myself from a kit. Wasn't quite so expensive that way."

"You're from a Smart District, aren't you? Is your daddy rich?"

"Yes, my parents are wealthy, and yes, I was born and grew up in Lidingö Smart District."

My temper gets the better of me. "I knew it, you spoilt brat."

"Listen up, old man, I've just saved your life. You should really wear a helmet when you ride your bike. Go on, feel your head."

I'm still annoyed, but do as I'm bidden. My fingers encounter a hard shell that covers my head from the top of my ears and upwards.

"Did I crack my skull?" I mumble bemused.

"In three places," she confirms. "You also have a fractured scaphoid in your right hand, and deep lacerations in both legs. I've stapled the lacerations and coated them in Hyper-Heal. They should be fine in a couple of hours. Your skull will take more time, probably three or maybe four days. The shell will detach by itself when the job's done. Luckily you have a very thick head. My scans haven't detected any haemorrhaging."

I remain silent for a few moments, attempting to digest what she's told me. Then I remember my stuff and begin to struggle to my hands and knees.

"Not yet!" she insists, but I ignore her. My things are scattered all over the place. The trailer is broken and my bike is nowhere to be seen.

"Did they take my bike?" I whisper.

"Yes, and some other items too, but I managed to save most of it."

This is too much. With bitterness, I recall the feeling I had of being a winner, and begin to cry.

"Oh no, don't be sad." The hard edge has left her voice. Despite feeling embarrassed I can't hold back the tears.

"Two steps forward, three steps back. I thought I'd broken that rule today. But life always seems to take more than it gives. Only a self-deluding old fool could fail to realise that."

"Come on now. You still have most of your possessions." She actually sounds as if she cares.

I probe my pockets with bruised fingers. The pendent from Moses is still there. Both Food and Thing-Source tubs are on the path, miraculously unbroken. Rummaging through the wreckage of the trailer I find the patterns for the smart-func jacket, lamb vindaloo, naan and merlot. A couple of metres away I spot the heater. There's a large crack in the shell. It's probably no longer functional.

The robbers got the wine kit, yeast, and the patterns for Chardonnay and Chicken Tikka Sizzler that I wanted for the lad's birthday. And they got my bike.

"A rich person like you can't understand what a bike means to somebody like me," I say quietly. "I traded today. It went really well. Thought I was a winner for once, but now that I've lost my bike... the day's been a disaster." I sigh. "Once a loser always a loser."

"That's something I want to change," she says. She comes to stand beside me and takes my hand. "Come and sit down. Let the medicines do their work and in a little while I'll help you get home with your stuff. Okay?"

I do as she says. To be honest, she seems genuinely decent. My body and head already hurt much less.

"While we wait, could I ask you about your life?"

"I dry my eyes, sniff and fix her with a wary look. "My life?"

"Will it be okay if I record our conversation?"

Now I'm really suspicious and my gratitude evaporates. "What for? And are you gonna pay me?"

"Pay you?" Her eyes flash with anger. "Have you any idea what these medicines cost?"

She has a point. "Okay, okay, but why do you want to record the interview, I mean if you're recording me it's not just a chat, right?"

She nods. "I'm a political scientist doing a doctorate in community development. I plan on dedicating my life to changing our society so ordinary citizens don't always need to *lose*, as you put it. That's why I'm out in the field. I need to speak to people, learn about their reality and how everything works. When I'm finished, I'm going to develop and implement improvement strategies."

I'm sorely tempted to make a snide comment about rich girls playing catcher in the rye, but there's an intensity in her eyes and a passion in her voice that stops me.

"If you succeed, you'll be the first for a very long time," I say. "Go on then, fire away."

She asks about my past. So, I tell her briefly about my background, the family, my chequered career, the periods of unemployment, and about my wife's death.

When I'm finished, she remains quiet for a while. "You know that the successive weakening of the state was unavoidable, don't you?" she says at last. "That it was largely due to technology in combination with demographics?"

My mood turns bolshie again. "Unavoidable. What do you mean, unavoidable? It was bad politics, pure and simple. Privatisation was the beginning of the end," I mutter. "Was that unavoidable?"

She draws in a deep breath as if to steel herself. "Well now, it really wasn't quite that simple."

"No?"

"By the time you moved here from England, the state was already finding it difficult to finance the same range of services it had delivered to previous generations."

"Corruption," I growled. "Appalling decisions and massive waste..."

"That was part of it, but not the whole story. Technical developments meant that there was so much more on offer, advances in medical treatments for example. And people naturally wanted access to all of it. Then there was the fall in childbirth and ageing generations that lived longer than ever before and needed constant state succour: pensions, loads of health care, residential homes etc, etc. So much was needed and so much became so much dearer."

She paused and seemed to be waiting for an answer, but I wasn't in the mood to provide one.

"New technology is expensive," she said. "Just as it becomes cheaper, another generation of technology appears to replace it. The state's range of services, in fact the state apparatus itself, shrank proportionately to the increased services on offer: social services and insurances. To begin with the wealthy gorged on new, enhanced services via private suppliers, while those less well-off consumed what the state still offered. But it was only a matter of time before the state's increasing poverty relative to that which was available meant its services no longer sufficed for anybody. Simply put, everybody had to buy supplementary services. Those who couldn't afford to, went without."

"That's it? These are the amazing insights of a PhD education?" I shake my head and mutter: "Thanks for the history lesson. In case you were in any doubt, my family belonged to those who went without."

She nodded. "But you were still better off than many out in the world. There was and still is a school, limited basic healthcare and so on. Some nations don't offer anything at all any more, others never did."

"Yeah, you're right now you mention it," I declare. "Three of us are still alive even... Listen, young lady, a prison cell, is no less a prison cell, just because you have a couple more cushions or it's a bit more spacious than the one down the corridor."

"Prison cell?"

"Yeah, prison cell. Take my son. A good lad. Very bright. Like his sister, bilingual from the start. He's a self-taught musician, for crying out loud. But have things gone well for him? No. He had concentration difficulties in school, wasn't good at national exams of the type they brought in for sixteen-year-olds. If the school had been able to offer him just a *little* more, he might have made it to college, might have got a job in one of the Smart Districts just as they were taking off.

"But state schools didn't have those resources, and private schools didn't want pupils who needed support because they cost more and costs reduce profit."

She raises her hands in a placatory gesture. "I know," she says softly, nodding again. But years of frustration are welling up inside me. I feel my face twist into a furious scowl and begin emphasising every word with a wagging finger,

"Poor bugger, that's what I say. Poor sod. His life has been crap. He didn't get to college, didn't get a start. He's never had what I'd call a *proper* job. Instead, to all intents and purposes he's been unemployed for most of his adult life. The limitations he's suffered were all external, imposed by a failed society and its so-called *systems*..."

"Yes," she agrees, "many people have been robbed of even basic opportunities for social mobility. But you make it sound as if it was planned that way. It wasn't. In Europe, we were getting poorer several decades before we realised what was going on. At the same time changes in technology meant a growing global range of services. But the state didn't have the resources to shoulder its responsibilities any more..."

"Aw, you've said that already. Technology, pah. What about the bloody *CCS*, how do you factor that into your thinking?"

"The what?"

"The Conservative-Counter-Strike, you know, the so-called backlash revolution? Things were already getting bad, but that's when it all really went off the rails: isolationism as opposed to internationalism, succession and devolution instead of global treaties and collaborations. Ring a bell?"

For the first time, she looks less certain. And I press home my advantage.

"Climate change denial, anti-science, anti-truth? We really took it in the teeth then; every sort of equality was eroded. Add that to your declining social insurance and welfare provision and the end of freedom of movement. Total smack down!"

"I know of it, of course," she says attempting to recover, "But to date the major focus of my studies has been the impact of technological change... as I was saying the state couldn't provide everyone with..."

"No, and so we just can't pull ourselves up from the foul-smelling sludge at the bottom of the river. The likes of you make me sick with your half-baked theories. As for the bloody state, it can take it where the sun don't shine."

I sit fuming, waiting for her to retaliate. But she's looking thoughtful again.

"Alright. Granted. But the state did what it could."

She's tenacious, I have to give her that.

"You live in state-owned accommodation, don't you? The politicians saw what was happening. When the exodus to new Smart Districts began and property rental companies went into receivership, the city bought all the historical buildings in central Stockholm for a pittance. That was a good move, wasn't it?"

I consider this for a few moments. She's right of course, but I still feel belligerent and don't want to concede any point.

"Our situation got a little bit better, I suppose," I admit without much grace. "But they should have done more! Look at the city as it is today. Most of the apartment blocks built in the mid-20th century have been demolished or are dilapidated beyond rescue. Only the old houses are still usable. There are massive empty gaps in the inner-city landscape and abandoned areas, like down at Hammarby, that are lawless."

"But they couldn't do any more," she insists. "They just didn't have the resources." She meets my furious gaze for a moment then shrugs and looks away. The gesture serves to make me more irritated than ever. I sense it's time to go in for the kill.

"Without the wave of decentralisation, things wouldn't have been so bad," I continue. "That's what really caused the decline of the old city."

She gazes straight into my eyes, a look of defiance on her face and I realise that she's far from beaten. "Yeah, I know," she says with quiet certainty. "And *technology* was the driving force behind that development. People didn't need to be physically present in the city to communicate, work or study. At the same time the Smart Districts were being established..."

"And they were supposed to save the world, the environment, and create jobs," I interrupt. "But as it turned out, only a select minority benefited. For the rest of us, New Vällingby and the likes were a big part of the problem!" I'd intended to regain the initiative, but as I speak emotion betrays me again. My vision blurs as tears fill my eyes. "You fucked everything up for the rest of us," I manage, but my voice is scarcely more than a husky whisper. She takes my hand. And despite an intense desire to hate her, I can't.

"The negative effects were unintentional, but you're absolutely right. The results have been a terrible disappointment. Personally, I am still captivated by the original vision, for a sustainable, just and smart society. Don't you think that's beautiful idea?"

I chuckle, without mirth. "Don't you know what paves the road to hell, young lady?" Old idioms like that are probably wasted on her, so I point to my broken trailer: "Look around you, where's the justice in this?"

She purses her lips and shrugs. "I agree."

"You do?"

"Yep. This is more than just my subject, you know. It's a passion. I've studied the process and its history in depth. Sadly, the results were remarkably similar throughout what we once called the industrialised world. Researchers and urban planners envisioned a boost for the whole community. The future would be environmentally-friendly, energy-saving with integrated infrastructure and advanced technology everywhere and in everything. In some parts of the world they built really big smart cities, housing entire multi-million citizen communities. Those have turned out to be the most successful. But for each integrated mega-city, there are huge numbers who live in shanty towns and tent camps outside. What happened here in the Nordics was a little different. With our individualistic traditions and history of small communities, existing urban centres fragmented into a plethora of micro-communities. And in the rush to meet the future there was a lack of coordination. Differing technical platforms and protocols were adopted causing compatibility issues between communities. Here in Sweden it was like a return to some sort of high-tech bronze age society of mini-states."

"But why?" I'm genuinely curious and put aside my desire to win arguments and punish rich kids for the moment.

"I'm not completely sure yet," she admits. "Maybe because financing was raised at county and municipal level. The money came from the private sector, it had to, because the state was broke. As ever, private money dictated the goals for these new communities. One result was that short-term investment returns were a lot higher up the agendas than establishing brave new altruistic utopias."

When she's finished, I don't say anything. What is there to add?

She looks at me. "How long have you lived on the Southside?"

"Over fifty years."

"Really. Want to know something? I like arguing with you. Can we stay in touch, for my studies I mean? Your perspective and knowledge could be pretty important."

I stare at her, trying to figure out if she's winding me up, but come to the conclusion that she probably isn't.

"Okay," I say and she records my mail address.

Then she begins fussing over my cuts and bruises. "How are you feeling? Hmm. These look good. I reckon we can get going now."

I abandon the broken trailer and we hang the buckets of Source under the bird drone. It's unbelievably powerful. The rest of the items we carry, but they don't weigh much and she seems very strong.

As we set off over New Årsta Bridge I realise that I'm really starting to warm to this young woman. She reminds me a bit of my daughter, both well-read and not afraid to enter the fray. In fact, she's a lot of fun. While we walk, I find myself answering her questions virtually without reserve or rancour.

"You must have some gratitude to the state for letting you live where you do at such low cost?"

"Gratitude, nah, I wouldn't say that. The state gets a fair bit for its subsidised rents," I reply with a grin.

"Do you really think so?"

"Of course. We're the ones who take care of what's left of the city."

"You?"

"Yep. Just think about it. These streets didn't cost the state very much. We live there, maintain the buildings, pay a bit of rent and our cooperatives keep the peace. We're the ones who hire the guard companies, not big brother state."

"Hmm, yes you do," she admits.

"Today the word is that the state took over for reasons of cultural history. But there are no police officers in these districts and state drones are few and far between. Besides they're usually busy elsewhere containing the 'problem'.

"When the state took over the historical properties in Högalid, Zinken and Tanto, they were rented out to 'reputable less well-off' folks. The key word was *reputable*. Poor people with a criminal past were excluded. I know because I've checked."

"So, you and your son are *reputable*?" She's grinning and I give her a warning look, but find it hard to suppress a smile.

"We just so happened to be living there already."

"Okay, but the state, via city hall, decided to let you take over?"

"I imagine they realised it would be better to collect a bit of rent, save the buildings that could be saved and maintain law and order. Our cooperatives are your Smart District's poorer cousins and a cheaper security solution than drones or police teams procured from private suppliers."

She thinks about my words. "Maybe you're right."

"I am," I announce without a trace of irony. "In a cooperative, everyone has an interest in keeping their nose clean. Because anyone who doesn't is expelled."

We reach the far side of the bridge and wander in safety to

Zinken's crossing. She's good enough to accompany me all the way back up to the flat, helping me on the stairs, where I come over a bit shaky.

The lad's home. As soon as I see him my tears return. "Sorry, son... I've lost the bike."

"Jesus, dad, look at you. Is that blood...? And your head!"

He hugs me and I can't help sobbing.

"Easy there, dad. Doesn't matter, mate. I'll sort the bike thing out, no problems, promise. Shit, look at the stuff you've brought, and you've a woman too. Just shows you're never too old, eh, you rascal."

I laugh despite myself and he leads me into the main room where I sit down on the edge of my bed. The day's excitement is catching up with me, and although my aches and pains have subsided, I feel giddy and a bit muddled as if I'm coming down with a fever.

In the kitchen, my new friend gives my son an account of what happened. He's grateful and tries to persuade her to stay for dinner, but her brother has already sent the car from Lidingö to fetch her. She promises there'll be other opportunities, however.

Later the lad and I are sitting together in the kitchen and I open a bottle of wine from our latest batch. It's made from fruit pulp and isn't bad when well-chilled, but it's nothing like the wines we used to be able to get.

"I'm sorry about today, son," I say again.

"Come on, dad, what for?" He's bent over the heater, fixing the crack with a disposable cold-welding wand.

"For losing the wine kit, son."

"Dad, we don't need wine kits any more. We've got a pattern for merlot and enough Food-Source to open our own restaurant."

He has a point.

"Just look at the stuff you managed to get for us. And by the way, I contacted Moses to say thanks and tell him what happened. He thinks he knows who your attackers were. I've given him our bike ident. As soon as they try to pass a guard post, or sell it, they're done for. Bloody amateurs."

I wonder if we'll get the bike back or if we'll have to buy a new one. Maybe Moses will help.

"There you go, good as new," he announces and places the heater on a ceramic coaster to protect the table beneath. He gets a briquette from the cupboard and fits it into the port. Before long I feel the temperature rising in the kitchen.

"Come on dad, it's my birthday in a few hours. How about we play that game we always used to when mum and sis were still around?"

I really don't want to, but feel I ought to indulge him.

"Okay."

He fetches the box, arranges the board on the table and shuffles the various decks of cards, placing them on the board. Then he positions our player figurines on their start squares. He's happier than I've seen him for a long time and so he should be: we have food, drink and he's going to work for Moses. A real job with a registered salary.

"I loved this game when I was a kid," he says, grinning. "Do you remember when the four of us used to play? You and mum always argued when your characters landed on the same square. Hah, and do you remember that time she killed you with her magic staff? You got so annoyed."

I smile at the memory. "They were good times, son. Even if I didn't fully realise it at the time." But he isn't listening.

"Just imagine if life was like this game," he says. "A throw of the dice and a world of adventure is at your feet. A whole world waiting to be explored, with chests of gold or jewels round every corner."

"Yes, that would be quite something," I agree in a weary voice. I reflect on the day, tallying up a sort of balance sheet in my head. Has it been a good one? Yes, on balance it has. Despite misadventures and losing the bike, my son has a job. A *job*! But we'll probably suffer setbacks tomorrow. That's how it works.

Then I think about my new acquaintance and wonder if she'll succeed in saving the future. I really hope so. Maybe the lad will get to experience some of the benefits before he's too old to enjoy them.

"What do you say, dad? Life's a bit like a game, isn't it? Instead of gold and magic swords, you can get jobs and Food-Source."

I nod and pour more wine. "But it's not a game I'm especially fond of."

"Aw, come on. You have to like it on a day like this?"

I take a big gulp from my glass and remain quiet for few moments, then I shake my head.

"It's a hard game son. Regardless of the good or bad served up on individual days, you're always gonna lose in the end."

God is a Weapon of Mass Destruction

Cynthia Atkins

*"This medal is for losing both your legs. This medal is for
being at the right place at the right time.
This medal is for your widow. This medal is for
everything. The frame is not included."*
—Seb Doubinksy

When you hear brass knuckles at the door—
You may think it is a scalper with tickets to
the blues show, but more like, *"Houston we
have a problem"*—Like a driver all hopped up
on Ambien or a 13 year old kid playing
a habit of video games. Where munition fantasies
are slagged in a trajectory of pithy old mongers
from a Japanese B-Movie. This manic driver follows
no rules of the road, nor engagement, only the rules
of bloody estrangement. In the back-seat,
GI-Joe & GI-Jane, sullen and lost into zippers
and buttons, rifling in muddy gardens of lusty flags.
When love is toxic it creates little snot-nosed
bombs and spoiled-rotten generals. Now, the bluesman
on the radio, says, *"he aint gonna play for dimes
no more, only for sobbing widows."* The billboard in
the clouds rains holy scriptures—Beauty with a license
to kill at every zealous church supper. Kids kneeling under desks,
not at them, in class rooms spewing ideology
with bullet points and sharpened pencils—Cocked
and loaded and powdered to the nines. *This is the right place
at the wrong time* in a factory of what-me-knots and bones.

The Hologram City

Preston Grassmann

The camera is the eye of a shark, floating over the pop-culture ruins of a Japanese market-town. Its predatory motions sweep over the neon reefs and sunken castles of a virtual sea, descending over aquatic themed shops and restaurants... the corporate avatars of fish and lamprey eels and goldfish... and too many goddamn Nemo. I try to close my eyes, but the candy-colored visions of the virtual sea still blaze in the sky of mind... and I feel sick again.

"You ok?" Rie asks.

"I've been out for too fucking long."

This one's definitely better than version 4.0."

"You mean Pokemon: City of Dead Streets." I suddenly see her face turn blue, an image of Squirtle rising into view.

Give me the broken bottles and the makeshift houses of the slum... the cracked concrete of the squalid suburbs... the rusted metal rods of unfinished buildings sprouting from the earth like dying plants, trying to grow back out into the world again. Give me anything but the dead VR worlds of the corporations.

"Prison was a step above that one," I say, barely exaggerating. It's only been two days since I've been out of the Virt-space prison cell, a coded world reduced into block ciphers and polygons. It had been designed to erode my sense of individuality, a method of reforming non-conformists like me. But they never accounted for Synaptic, the drug that fused itself to the DNA and offered me a private, alternative existence.

I turn to see one of my old haunts, a record-store called Lighthouse, turned into a Cosplay shop. Gothic Lolita's in short skirts, who know nothing of Nabakov, beckon beneath a sign that reads Rust and Stardust. *The breaking of a wave cannot explain the whole sea.*

Fuck this place. Fuck the fucking fuck, as an old friend used to say.

"Why the hell are clothing shops so popular in Virt-space?" I ask. Outside of VR, the clothing in Rust and Stardust are just a collection of gray and white dresses hanging from rusted metal racks. Since every fucking thing is covered over in Virt-space, what purpose does it serve?

"It's about how they feel, the texture of the fabric," she says. "It's the only sense most of them have left."

In the distance, a group of policemen are staring into the crowd. Synaptic offers the image of grouper-fish huddled together among the rocks, waiting to pluck the remains of dead icons from the pop-culture abyss. If only.

"You know, when I was a kid, all I wanted was to escape into virtual worlds."

"Now you want to find your way out of them. Are you sure this plan of yours is gonna work?"

You think I'm a hack?"

"No, but you're a hacker," she says. "And the sharks never stop moving." She points to the approaching drones.

We turn on the holograms embedded in our clothes and they spring outward into tentacles and the tapered heads of cephalopods. Now, I can barely see her summer-dress and sandals, her black hair dyed into streaks of purple.

What do you know about holograms, Commissioner?

It was something I had said during the interrogation. The Police Commissioner had been leaning back in his chair with a satisfied smile, certain that he had accomplished everything he had set out to do. A framed image of a hologram rose had been on his desk.

"No matter how many times you cut them up, you can still see the whole image in each piece."

"That's the problem with your books and movies... you get too many ideas in your head. Our society can't function with scumbags like you in it. You will be cited for Civil Disobedience..."

I began quoting from Thoreau's Civil Disobedience:

The mass of men serve the state thus, not as men mainly, but as machines, with their bodies.

He had stood up then and slapped me across the face.

They are the standing army, and the militia, jailors, constables, posse comitatus, etc. In most cases there is no free exercise whatever of the judgment or of the moral sense...

He struck me in the stomach with his baton and leered as he stood over me.

"We have to go," Rie says, bringing me back to the present.

I switch out of Virt-space, the vision of barracuda and sharks changing back into what they are—police drones scanning the crowd.

I feel relief in the dirt, where the streets are worn with the grime of its own history, with broken shop-fronts and old, lightless signs hanging in rusted frames. A boy leans against a wall, reading a battered comic, a dog barks under the eaves of a makeshift house, a young woman on a rooftop flips off the passing drones. The holdouts and the exiles live here, and for me, its home.

"We're almost there," she says.

We pass through alleys filled with non-VR bars and restaurants, under a ragged tunnel of leaning signs. Here is a quiet street filled with love hotels, clientele scurrying between them. For a moment, Synapse summons the image of crabs, but I force them to scurry into the shadows of rocks.

The sounds of the city fade into the steady hum of converging drones.

"You're in violation...," a voice suddenly calls out, cascading through the speakers of a drone, but it begins to sputter, shifting into my opening act of Civil Disobedience:

but they put themselves on a level with wood and earth and stones; and wooden men can perhaps be manufactured that will serve the purpose as well.

The drones move frantically above, as if trying to gather back into formation. Some collide or fall against the grid-work of signs above.

Such command no more respect than men of straw or a lump of dirt.

They have the same sort of worth only as horses and dogs. Yet such as these are commonly esteemed good citizens.

In violation of statute 757..." another drone calls out, but it screeches into a sound that I hear as mrmee, mrmee, mrmee and then:

Others—as most legislators, politicians, lawyers, ministers, and officeholders—serve the state chiefly with their heads; and, as they rarely make any moral distinctions, they are as likely to serve the Devil, without intending it, as God.

"It's working," Rie says, nodding at the people around us, holding up battered copies of banned books and magazines, old record covers, newspapers and comics. We can feel the energy around us gathering, and we make our way through the crowds and around buildings, until we reach the border of our new town, an island in the midst of the Tokyo ruins. The Hologram City springs up around us, each district a literary reference to outlawed books. In Ballard, sea-weed drapes window frames, hanging from signs and billboards like a mockery of its Virtspace version. Plankton swirls in the air, floating in the space between us. Above the buildings, broad beams of light spill between the hollows of coral-towers, cascading down as if through the surface of the sea.

The next hacked drone hovers above the crowd and begins to recite from The Drowned World:

all the way down the creek, perched in the windows of the office blocks and department stores, the iguanas watched them go past, their hard frozen heads jerking stiffly... ... Without the reptiles, the lagoons and the creeks of office blocks half-submerged in the immense heat would have had a strange dream-like beauty, but the iguanas and basilisks brought the fantasy down to earth.

As we enter Burroughs, holograms of Marrakech bars begin to appear, balconies full of flowers, a tethered goat in an alley, mugwumps huddled over stools or standing beneath the broken-stone monuments of exotic cities. Here, the parties have already begun, celebrants lifting glasses to the sky, quoting their favorite passages, watching movies on the abandoned screens of an older city. As a drone passes overhead, everyone stops to listen to the voice they have come to celebrate:

You must not lose faith in humanity. Humanity is an ocean. If a few drops of the ocean are dirty, the ocean does not become dirty.

There are policemen wandering through the area, but they are staring at each other in confusion. They know that something is wrong, that they no longer have control, but it will take them time to realize its source. *What do you know about holograms, Commissioner?*

"Congratulations," she says, her lips sparking against my ear.

This is just the beginning," I say. We pass through the hologram towns of Kobo Abe and Ryu Murakami, crowds gathering at each one, waiting for the drone-readings to begin.

Samarqand is concealed from view by the projection of a blue-tiled mausoleum dome. This is the place where the resistance had begun, where all the planning and preparation was done. I can still remember the streets filled with protesters struggling against the government bans, where we fought against the controls and fire-walls of censors. Back then, we built hidden spaces in Virt, digital safe-rooms where we stashed our copies of outlawed books and movies. But now, we hide them in plain sight. I see battered copies of White City's and Goodbye Babylon's and Spontaneous Combustions, pages worn and frail with time, and I almost weep at the sight.

"Welcome back," Kitano says at the door. I embrace him for a moment, watching the gray and white tattoos of sharks slide back and forth across his fore-arms.

"Have you seen our old friends?" I ask.

"They're all waiting for you," he says, tilting his head in the direction of the stairs. He smiles to Rie, handing her a hard-copy flyer of the readings. "It's good to see you again."

Rie holds a tip near his hand, watching the sharks gather hungrily around it. "Nice tattoos," she says, as she puts it in his open palm, the sharks pretending to tear away at it like a meal.

From down below, I hear the sound of familiar voices, the

MC announcing another reading. I can feel the old joy of our revolution again, the unity of our cause.

As we descend the stairway, it's as if we're sinking into the depths of the sea, a stream of bubbles flowing up from volcanic rocks and hypothermal vents. The center of the stage is lit in flashes of faded orange light, as if this is the primordial birth of a new world. The illusion is broken only by the bookshelves and stacks of records surrounding the room, each filled with outlawed artifacts. I see part of the old crew sitting at a table next to the stage, bodies and faces barely visible beneath avatars of Bush Vipers and Thorny Dragons and Goblin Sharks. As I reach the table, Rie points up at screens that show an overhead view of Shibuya. "Drone-perspectives," she says.

The screen shows the crowd emerging out of VR, staring at the city around them in confusion.

Some are frightened by the change. Others are moving in the direction of The Hologram City, drawn by the cheering crowds and the readings. They pass by stores and shops no longer augmented by their corporate sponsors. The police are running between the buildings, unsure of where to go, urging people to remain calm.

Silence settles over the crowd as new drones move into view, spreading out above the city. The image of a rose appears in each one.

"I'd like to welcome our first reader tonight... He joins us all the way from Denmark... " and the crowd is standing, cheering him on as his voice resounds across the city:

The night was cold and beautiful, the stars crowning the black sky like a hierophant. It all hung like a beautiful tapestry....

As he reads, the rose holograms begin to join, forming a single flower over the city.

No matter how many times you cut them up, you can still see the whole image in each piece...

King

Paul Schwartz

The Queen opened the door and marched through the room
with her hands at her hips, fingers curled like deformed fortune
cookies. A man's world they say—
Menstrual heart hoof-beating, toxic-shock excreting
A simple lie we tell them
The women's clay we crave

The king of it all declares—
A man's world we say!

Germ warfare, no retreating, mothers homemade preheating
Fragile sarcophagus a-bleeding
Lies forever feeding,
Menstrual heart hoof-beating, toxic-shock excreting
A simple lie we tell them
We reserve truth only for the brave

The king knows

Her room was ripped apart, the diorama of course, was gone.
Clothes everywhere, stereo pried with something.
The masks were still back behind the cardboard box of typewriter
paper in her closet.
He grabbed them both and put them in the little compartment
for holding paper in the bottom of his typewriter

Fear-motivation

A man's world they say?
King starts—

Febrile dreams in flourished breeding
Of breach births and cot-death pleading,
The novel not worth reading
Germ warfare, no retreating, mothers homemade preheating
Fragile sarcophagus a-bleeding

Lies forever feeding,
Menstrual heart hoof-beating, toxic-shock excreting
A simple lie we tell them

He pulled myself upright by the fibers of the carpet when the smoke disappeared as it does, at its own strange rate. He had to grab his own head and position it too, like a sphere jangling in a jar of syrup.

Simple hormonal hallucinations, eh?
King will do anything to prove his mantra
Beyond the range of experiment

Elements

James Goddard

Earth

Oliver had been obsessed with being thought of as a good man ever since his youth. Before he was old enough to vote he'd joined a voluntary organization that looked after the gardens of those who could no longer manage it for themselves. This choice, in a way, determined the course of his life.

Academically bright, instead of going to a conventional university and becoming a historian or a geographer, he'd opted instead to attend an agricultural college, and the horticultural courses in particular. He learned all about plants, their seasons, and how to keep a garden looking colourful at any time of year. By the time he graduated he already had a guaranteed position as an under-gardener at a stately home where he'd helped out during his summer breaks.

Palace House, Beaulieu, was, among the great stately homes, on the small side to be sure, but to him it was exquisite. Whereas the larger stately homes often verged on the ostentatious, and displayed a vulgarity that was almost tawdry, Beaulieu was still like a real family home. Its owner, Lord Montagu, could often be found mingling with the tourists who went to visit the house, or the extensive collection of vintage cars in the nearby Motor Museum.

One morning, Lord Montagu greeted his new gardener in the formal garden; he was a friendly man who carried his lineage with casual ease and had no need of airs and graces. He offered his hand for Oliver to shake, as soiled as his hands were, and asked him what his ambition was. Oliver thought for a moment before replying.

"I think my ambition is to be remembered as a good man, Your Lordship," he said.

Lord Montagu looked puzzled, then he smiled, instructed him to keep up the good work, thanked him and walked on.

Oliver remained at Palace House for almost seven years. During that time, he learned the practical side of garden design, as well as all the tricks of the gardening trade. He felt, at last that he was ready to make his way in the world as a hands-on garden designer. In his mind he was convinced that those of lesser means than Lord Montagu, would pay handsomely to have their gardens redesigned by someone who had been a gardener for His Lordship.

As things turned out, he was right. He had done very well for himself, he owned a nice house, a nice car (as well as his business vehicles) and took holidays in interesting places; but he had never married and had no children. Now he thought he was too old to marry and raise a family, instead he fulfilled himself by doing good things, but in a very discreet way.

He supported local charities for the disabled, the blind and the homeless, each of which was delighted to receive quite large donations from a mysterious benefactor several times a year. He remembered how his own parents had struggled, and anonymously replaced worn out household appliances for poor families of the town. Women cried when a new washing machine or cooker arrived unexpectedly at their doors. He anonymously organised and paid for a day trip to the seaside each summer, for children from the orphanage. He felt proud of these achievements. He was being a good man.

A few friends knew of his largesse and often asked him why he didn't use his money to buy a villa on the Mediterranean coast or a hideaway in Florida.

"I have everything I want here. I don't need to own a house in the sun to take a good holiday. My home is comfortable. I even have a swimming-pool and a real home-cinema room with comfortable seats and a giant screen. What more do I want. Doing good for the benefit of others is my pleasure, so I'm being quite selfish when I help the needy. I like doing good. I want to be remembered as a good man."

As the years passed, his fortune grew, the money he didn't

use to do good, he invested wisely. He built a chain of garden centres that were phenomenally successful, he developed, packaged and sold his own varieties of seeds; but despite his success his real work was still gardening. None of his clients knew that he was a multi-millionaire businessman when he dug trenches, hefted rocks around and cut down trees in their gardens—he was just Oliver, the garden designer and gardener who had been recommended to them.

There came a time in Oliver's life when his age touched sixty, just as it does for most of us. He began to take stock of his life, he examined his success, thought deeply about his good works, and wondered if he had really been good enough. He tried to think of new ways to do good, and worried when he had no ideas.

To take his mind off this problem, he picked up the latest package from the Forgotten Films Club, he'd been a member ever since he'd set up his home cinema; the club specialised in films that were forgotten, most of them weren't very good, though occasionally he watched one that he thought was a real gem. This month's selection was *Walter: the Story of a Life*; it had been made in 1954 and Oliver had never heard of the director or any of the cast. At the end of the film a shadowy and indistinct figure watched a group of people in what appeared to be beautiful, wide-lawned parkland.

Walter was a successful businessman who became obsessed with the need to do good, and, as he watched, Oliver recognised that his own life mirrored that of Walter in many, many ways. Walter's solution for dealing with his large fortune was to set up a charitable foundation, and emulating that became Oliver's big idea.

Over the next several weeks, Oliver discussed his idea with his financial adviser, his banker and his lawyer, all of whom thought it was a bad idea. Their reaction proved to him that setting up the Good Man Charitable Foundation had to be his priority. Supporting, in perpetuity, the causes that he already supported anonymously, was to be the main objective of his foundation. Oliver realised, however, that the many hundreds of millions he had invested would generate more than enough income for that, so his foundation was to have the freedom to seek new groups of people to help, provided only that the foundation's choices were compatible with the principles he enshrined in its constitution.

All of Oliver's investments were transferred to the Good Man Charitable Foundation, a board of trustees was appointed, and staff hired to manage the charity. He retained control of his businesses for the time being, although that too would pass to his foundation upon his death.

He continued to live as a very wealthy man for almost twenty years, and still had sufficient funds to commit to individual acts of kindness. His foundation grew into a behemoth among charities, and its helping hands encircled the globe. As he monitored its progress, without interfering, he felt very proud. He felt, in fact, that he had at last achieved that great and good thing for which he had been born among men. When that thought registered, Oliver breathed his last and died peacefully in his sleep.

His funeral service was a humanist one, there were none of the trappings of religion. His coffin, on his instructions, was made of sturdy cardboard that would quickly rot away in the ground. While still alive he'd purchased a field adjacent to the local cemetery, and had designed and landscaped it as a garden of peace where anyone could sit in silent contemplation. A corner of that garden was his last resting place on earth.

No mausoleum was to be raised to commemorate his life and good works and his grave marker was to be a simple granite slab. What was inscribed on that slab, if anything, Oliver left to others. His final wish had been for his coffin to be aligned so that his face looked towards a tree covered rise a short distance away.

Looking down from that rise was a shadowy and indistinct figure among the trees. It watched a small gathering of invitees with bowed heads around the grave. It couldn't hear the words spoken by the speaker, but hoped they were simple words. After a few minutes, those around the grave each picked up a handful of soil and let it trickle through their fingers onto the simple coffin. Then they moved slowly away. The figure watched as the gravediggers shovelled the mound of earth back into the hole. When that was finished, they moved a slab of stone into place, it was wider than the grave itself and was supported by the solid ground on either side. Their work finished, the two men moved off to dig another hole or mow the cemetery lawns or whatever else gravediggers did when not digging graves.

That was the end of Oliver—but for one last thing. From among the trees the shadowy and indistinct figure drifted down to the graveside. It was Oliver of course, or a version of him. He looked down at his grave marker, read the words inscribed there:

Oliver ----------
1959—2039
A Good Man

He was pleased with the words, very pleased, proud even, but he found the gilt with which they were lined both showy and inappropriate.

Air

When she was growing up, Sarah loved the outdoors. She spent so much time among the trees in the large garden of her family home, that her mother told her that she should have been born as one of the woodland folk. She'd had no idea what that meant when she was seven or eight years old; the only woodland folk she knew of were in the stories in her colourful childhood books. They were small, happy people whose clothing was made from flower petals and leaves. They wore acorn cups as hats. Even the adults spent most of their time playing among the trees with their friends the birds and butterflies.

As she grew older she realised that the woodland folk weren't real, that there was no fairyland utopia among the trees, no place were laws were not necessary because everyone was so honest and nice. By the time she was old enough to go into town by herself, her mother had warned her of darker things; don't walk through the woods if the sun isn't shining, never tread on someone else's shadow, never, ever talk to strangers, don't breathe in another's breath. She laughed, and told her mother not to worry, told her that she would be careful. In reality, though, she did just as all teenagers everywhere do, and that was exactly what she wanted. She walked through the woods rain or shine, because it was the shortest route to the bus stop; she trod on the shadows of others because it seemed silly to avoid doing so, she talked to strangers—especially if they were cute boys.

She always thought the prohibition on talking to strangers was a bit silly. If you never talk to strangers, she reasoned, you would only ever talk to your own family, you would never have friends or meet anyone new. She never said this to her mother, of course. Had she done so, she would have been punished for being rude or cheeky. Her mother had been very strict with her once her father had left. When he lived with them, he had managed to control her mother's anger and she had rarely been punished.

"You will understand one day, Sarah, and that's enough. Don't ask me about it again." Her mother had said when Sarah asked why daddy wasn't at home any more.

She didn't see her father again until she was fifteen, and even then it was in secret. She saw a man waiting by the school gate, and she recognised him instantly. Her memory of him hadn't dimmed in the seven years since they'd last been together. Then he had just been daddy, now, as she rushed towards him, arms outstretched, she thought he looked quite handsome.

"Who's this then, Sarah?" One of her school friends asked with a wink that might have been interpreted as having salacious intent.

"It's my da… it's my father, I mean."

"I didn't think you had a father."

"Of course I have a father, stupid. Everyone has a father somewhere—or had a father," she suddenly remembered that her friend's mother had been widowed two years earlier.

Her father was smiling in the way she remembered, with deep lines from the corners of his nose to the corners of his wide, red-lipped mouth. She wrapped her arms around him, hugged him and began to cry.

"Daddy, daddy, daddy," she sobbed over and over. "Where were you daddy? Where were you?"

It was as if she was a child again. She felt the warmth of his body through his clothing, felt his strength. His arms went around her, hugged her as she hugged him. She reached up and stroked his cheek, felt the stubble of his beard. She looked at his face, and saw his smiling eyes, they glistened with tears that didn't flow. She felt his warm breath against her cheek and breathed deeply of it.

As she was lost in welcoming her father back into her life she lost track of her homeward routine. She forgot there was a bus to catch, friends to laugh and joke with. Someone called her name, but it was distant, disconnected, meant for another Sarah, not the Sarah she was at that moment. Someone walked quickly by, brushed against her, grabbed her arm in passing. Sarah stumbled as she was pulled, let go of her father and turned, surprised to see the school bus waiting, its engine running.

"Quick... the bus," a voice said, it was her best friend.

Sarah was unwillingly pulled along. When she twisted her head to look back, her father was gone.

"Who was that old man you were cuddling? Too old for you, must be a perv."

"He's not old and he's my dad. And I wasn't cuddling him, I was hugging him." She was sure there was a difference between cuddling and hugging, but she wouldn't have been able to explain what it was.

When she reached home, she didn't mention to her mother that she had seen her father. She knew that was a shortcut to a row, and the happiness inside her didn't want a row tonight. Her mother had prepared a make-do meal, from odds and ends left over from other meals, she was lucky to get even that. It was date night and soon her mother would be gone, she would be left alone to do whatever she wanted to do. She had homework, but when that was done all she wanted to do was think about her dad.

Somehow she knew he was there with her, in the very air she breathed. She could still smell him, still feel him. Without knowing why, she began to sob, but they were happy tears she was shedding. She was happy. She was happy. She had found her father.

Over the next two years she hugged her father a few more times outside the school gates. He was just there as she rushed towards the bus. She stopped, they hugged for what seemed like ages. His solidity, his hands, the air around him were all building blocks of her happiness. She moved towards the bus. When she looked he was gone. It was always like that. It didn't seem odd to her that they never spoke to each other, such was the love she felt, from her to him, from him to her, that words didn't seem necessary.

At home, her life had become almost unbearably miserable, rows with her mother, rows with Piggy, her mother's boyfriend Roland, whose nickname came from his greed. To Sarah, it seemed that her presence in the house was something they didn't want, she was tolerated due to whatever sense of duty her mother still felt.

After one particularly bad row, Sarah, feeling that she could no longer tolerate her situation, stuffed a few things into a backpack, and headed for the door.

"I'm off," she said. "You'll see me when you see me, if ever, that is."

"Don't you talk to me like that, young lady," her mother screeched, as Piggy held her at the waist from behind and smirked as he kissed her neck. "Where are you going?"

From the doorstep, Sarah looked back.

"I'm going to stay with dad. I've been meeting him for two years or more." she blurted out without really meaning to. She had no idea where her father lived.

Her mother's face changed from rage to sadness, her arms spread imploringly.

"Sarah dear, come back. Please. Please come back."

Sarah dashed for the gate and into the darkness, hearing her mother call "I have to tell you something, Sarah. Please come back." As she went.

Somehow, in the darkness, Sarah made her way to a friend's

house and asked if she could stay the night. She had no idea where her father lived, and decided she would look for him in the morning.

"I told my mum where I was going," she said, after explaining that they'd had a row about nothing really, while Piggy goaded her mother to greater excesses of wounded pride and indignant anger than Sarah had ever experienced before. "It will give us both a chance to cool off."

Next morning, she began looking for her father, but no one in the village, and no one in the town, who might have known where he was, had any idea of his whereabouts. One or two family friends, people her mother hadn't seen for ages, looked at her in a puzzled way, but said nothing. Finally, after four days of looking, four days without success, she decided it was time to go home again. Her friend's family had been very kind, but she felt that she could stay in their home no longer. She was surprised that the police hadn't gone around the village trying to find her, knocking on doors, asking questions. That, she thought, was the measure of her mother's lack of interest in her. She wasn't looking forward to the coming confrontation.

She dawdled along the village street, turned off into the woods; the ground was squidgy from recent rain, her shoes were covered with mud, but she didn't care. She saw shadows moving among the trees, but she wasn't afraid, she'd seen them often. They were harmless. Maybe they were the woodland folk. The thought made her smile, it was a small smile, a fleeting smile, but it was real.

"I'm glad you're going back to mum," a man's voice said, a voice so soft it might have been nothing but a movement of air. "She's not perfect, but you need each other."

Sarah turned in a full circle, there was no one to be seen, but in the air was her father's fragrance, a scent of aftershave, of toothpaste, of cigars. For a moment she felt sad, then happiness washed over her, tears of happiness streamed from her eyes. Laughing, came out of the woods and crossed the road, she saw her mother waiting at the door, smiling. Then, still laughing, she opened the garden gate.

Fire

Each morning, when he awoke, Lynton got out of his bed, went to the en-suite bathroom and showered, brushed his teeth, flossed and shaved. He dried himself, dried his hair and applied a small amount of hair gel—enough to keep him looking smart throughout the day—and combed his hair. He sprayed deodorant beneath his arms and applied cologne lightly to his cheeks and neck. When he was satisfied that the morning ritual was completed as well as he could complete it, he returned to his bedroom and selected his clothes for the day. He liked coordinated colours, so to go with his dark blue business suit he chose a pale blue shirt, an un-patterned brown tie and dark blue socks, the colour of his underwear didn't bother him, although it was usually white.

When he was dressed to his satisfaction, he carefully folded his suit jacket over his left arm and went down to the kitchen. Since Jennifer had left him six months earlier, no aroma of cooking bacon greeted him, no smell of fresh coffee, no cheery good morning or kiss on the cheek. Sometimes he missed that.

He and Jennifer were still friends, but she had decided that living together didn't work for her. She told Lynton that he was too punctilious in his habits, too careful in his choice of words. She said there was nothing spontaneous about him and that meant there were no surprises in their relationship. She said that sometimes he annoyed her with his predictability. He argued that if that was so he would change, but he didn't change, and six weeks later they had the same conversation again—almost verbatim. When he returned from work that day, Jennifer had packed her things and left. There was no note.

For the first two or three weeks after Jennifer left, he felt more alone than he had for many years, but gradually his life had settled down again, and he convinced himself that the very things that had caused Jennifer to leave, his punctiliousness, his routines, were the things that had helped him get through their separation.

A month passed before he heard from Jennifer. His 'phone rang and when he answered it was her voice he heard. She was worried about him. She hoped he was alright. She hoped he was remembering to eat properly. Maybe they could have dinner together, not yet, but soon. They both refrained from asking the other if they were seeing anyone else. After that she called him at least once a week, but would always withhold her number and refuse to give an address.

As he waited for fresh coffee to splutter through the grind-and-brew machine he had bought, he crossed to the fireplace and took a photograph from the mantelpiece above. It was a picture of Jennifer of course, she was smiling and her auburn hair, though unmoving in the picture, danced around her face. He stared at the picture fondly, how he still longed for her presence, her touch, her soft, warm laughter. Then he kissed the picture and replaced it on its shelf above the fireplace.

Getting his dustpan and brush from the kitchen he bent over and carefully swept up the light grey ash and small curls of burnt paper that were on the hearth. That too had become a morning ritual. He had no idea where the ash came from, the fire was electric and nothing burned there except ersatz flames. In an unusually contemplative moment he wondered if his passion for Jennifer had somehow burst into physical form without him noticing, had burned for a moment and fallen as ash, but he knew it was a ridiculous notion.

His daily life was neither happy nor sad. He had friends, he had things to do and places to go—and he had his work. Days, weeks and months passed and he knew a kind of contentment, but always it was anticipating a call from Jennifer that gave him the most pleasure. After they'd spoken, after her voice was gone and the 'phone was replaced on its cradle, he always felt a sense of anti-climax, a bereftness that didn't pass away until he'd fallen asleep that night and awoken again the next morning—then he felt an emptiness that needed to be filled by his own busyness.

When he didn't hear from Jennifer for two weeks in succession, he began to worry. He worried for Jennifer, thinking that something might have happened to her, and he worried himself because his routine was interrupted, and he disliked it intensely when that happened.

Two weeks became three and three became four, and he reasoned that Jennifer had found someone else. That was terrible for him, but he still had her photograph, he still hoped.

As he stood there, dustpan in hand, he picked up the photograph of Jennifer again, kissed it again, replaced it again. That was a break in his routine, and his actions annoyed him.

★★★

Another six months passed and Lynton became more and more obsessed with the small rituals that dominated his life. They were unimportant, he knew that, but he couldn't alter his habits. On the few occasions that he'd tried to do things differently, something bad happened; perhaps he spilled coffee on himself, or almost had an accident driving his car, or forgot to do something important at work and had to explain himself to his obnoxious manager. For these things he always blamed his breaks with routine, and the next day he returned to his punctilious ways and the world was alright again.

One morning, while he was eating the breakfast of muesli and Greek yoghourt that he always ate, he saw his photograph of Jennifer burst into flames. His first reaction was disbelief. This couldn't happen. It wasn't supposed happen. It wasn't part of his routine. By the time these thoughts had passed through his mind, the flames had gone and pale grey ash and small curls of burned paper were drifting down to the hearth. Only when he had finished his breakfast did he cross to the fireplace to look.

He'd already cleared the hearth of ash once that morning, as he always did, but he went to the kitchen and returned with his dustpan and brush, then he carefully swept up the ash.

It was not in him to be alarmed or surprised by what he had witnessed, but at least he thought he now knew where the ash in the hearth came from. Any explanation as to how the photograph caught fire each night and then was whole again next morning wasn't his concern. It was just something that happened. He disposed of the ash, replaced the dustpan and brush in the cupboard and was drying his hands after washing his breakfast dishes, when the doorbell rang. Another break with routine, and it bothered him.

★★★

A few minutes later, when the policeman had left, Lynton put on his jacket, locked the house door and went to work. He drove as he always did, but he was at least ten minutes late.

He thought about what the policeman had told him. He knew he would never see Jennifer again, even her photograph had failed to reappear. He knew he would never hear her voice again as well. Those were things he had already accepted, even before the policeman's visit.

He thought he should feel sad that Jennifer had died in a house fire. He thought he should want to understand why it had taken more than five months to identify her remains. He thought he should want to know how the police had found out about his relationship with Jennifer. But those things were not a part of any one of his routines, and he let the thoughts drift away. He would miss the photograph of Jennifer though, that was a break with routine he would need to factor into his life.

Water

It wasn't so much that she was lonely, not in any real sense. She had plenty of friends in the town, they invited her out and visited often. They made sure that her life was full, just as good friends should. She spent very little time alone, and when she was alone she played music quite loudly, or turned the television on, so that it drowned out the silence and it wasn't as if she was alone. Sooner or later Peter returned from work, the music or TV were turned down, or switched off, and she wasn't alone any more.

She would prepare their evening meal, the simple, wholesome food that Peter loved. They would talk and laugh. Sometimes, after dinner, they walked along their quiet street until they came to the pub on the corner. It was called The Waggoner's Arms, but there was no coat of arms on the swinging sign and the origins of the name were lost to time. Inside, they met people they knew and talked about unimportant things to an accompaniment of raucous laughter. Peter drank best bitter and sneered at anyone who ordered lager, a boys' drink he called it, she drank white wine spritzers. When the landlord called 'last orders' they dawdled back to their comfortable home, a home made from Peter's hard work and perspiration—and her own feminine skills. Then they would drink Ovaltine, or not—depending on their mood, and go to bed. It was a routine. It was their routine, and it suited them very well.

Each morning, except Saturdays and Sundays, they got up at around seven. She made breakfast, while Peter prepared himself for work. He was a teacher. He taught carpentry skills at a local college. After he left the house, after she watched him climb into their car and slam its door, after he reversed out into the street and drove away, always with a little tooting of the cars horn, she went back into the house. There, she cleared away the breakfast things as loud music played from the radio in the kitchen, did the washing up, perfunctorily dusted and tidied their living room. When that was done, she went upstairs to the bedroom.

She sat on the edge of the bed and stared down at the small pool of water on the wood-laminate floor. It was always on her side of the bed, never on Peter's, so he always failed to notice it.

Every morning it was there, with one or two isolated drops trailing away to the bedroom door. The first time she had noticed the water it puzzled her, but she simply grabbed some Kleenex from the box on her bedside cabinet and wiped the spill away. By later in the day she had forgotten all about it. That's how it was for the first few weeks the water was there, but gradually she began to wonder where it came from. She never mentioned it to Peter, she knew he would worry about a leaking roof or a leaking pipe in the attic, even though there was no damage to the ceiling.

Months passed, and wiping away the water became just another part of her morning routine, but its routineness didn't stop her wondering. One day she decided to go to the library, there she used a computer to research spontaneous appearances of water. There were a few mentions of strange occurrences like the appearance of here water, there reports, too, of statues crying and water flowing from ancient walls or solid rock. Without exception these manifestations were interpreted as signs from God. She didn't believe in god and so couldn't accept such explanations. Although she liked the idea of crying statues, they had no statues at home. When she left the library to meet a friend for lunch, she had, essentially, learned nothing.

The following morning, she was still thinking of a statue that cried, and tears were very much on her mind. As she sat on the edge of their bed, she leaned forward and dipped a finger into the water near her feet. She sniffed at her moist fingertip, but there was no odour that she could detect. Then she cautiously dabbed her finger onto her tongue, and instantly tasted the slight salinity of the water. To be certain, she repeated the experiment, and yes, there was a slight saltiness to the water.

Tears, she thought, I have tears beside my bed. She knew it was irrational. She knew it was impossible, unless… She let the thought tail off, it was getting uncomfortably close to the thing they never mentioned, the thing her friends never mentioned, a great sadness in her, in their lives, that they had successfully built an emotion-proof mental wall around.

Still she said nothing to Peter about the water.

Her life continued, she kept busy, she laughed a lot, she went out a lot, she joined a gymnasium where she made new friends. She was happy and contented with her life, or so she thought. Every now and then, however, her thoughts turned dark and the thing they never mentioned began to demolish the wall in her mind.

During a restless night's sleep, perhaps nine months after the water first appeared, she heard a sound that frightened her. It was a very soft sound, but when she strained her hearing to catch it, it was so mournful, so bereft of hope that it made her want to weep. After about ninety seconds, and with her eyes, she knew brimming with tears, she nudged Peter until he woke up.

"Do you hear that?" She asked, her voice barely able to hold back its sobs. "Do you hear that, Peter?"

Peter was silent for a moment.

"I hear nothing," he said.

"You don't hear that child crying?"

"It's probably just an insect outside."

"No," she said, "it's here, in this room."

"I can't hear anything except your voice. Let me sleep, please, please."

"I thought it might be… " she said.

"Don't start that again, we're over it. It does no good, no good at all, to dwell on what happened."

They both fell silent, and by and by sleep came to them. Even in the grip of tiredness, neither of them actually mentioned the thing they never mentioned.

ext morning, Peter said nothing about their mild nocturnal altercation. She thought he had probably forgotten it already.

After he left the house, after she watched him climb into their car and slam its door, after he reversed out into the street and drove away, with a little tooting of the cars horn, she did the things she always did, like a good and dutiful wife. When she reached the bedroom she sat on the bed just as she always did, then she tasted the salt water on the floor as had become her habit. She began to cry.

She thought about their daughter. Emma had been six years old when she left the world. An illness without a name had taken her. She had died in a hospital bed.

"Thank you mummy," she had whispered with her last breath.

It had taken two years for them to get over the loss, two years for their child's death to become the thing they never mentioned.

She lost track of the time as she sat on the bed.

"Emma," she said over and over, "is that you darling. Are you here. Talk to me darling."

Outside the sun shone, the birds sang. She heard mail drop onto the doormat, she heard the telephone ring.

In their bedroom though, was only silence, in her was only pain and emptiness.

On the floor, by her feet, the little pool of water was fed by her own tears.

Bathyscape Blues

Phil Breach

The porthole is but seven inches wide. Hunched before its
pachydermal pane,
I gaze upon the ruin of outside,
the circle blurred by greasy, streaking rain.
She's called the Belemnite, this rusting hulk.
We hang above the roiled soiled sea, shaking in the belly of her
bulk,
Jarring down by ratcheted degree. We make the waves.
She hits and rolls and sinks, bowling us with bile-rising
motion.
Somewhere up above a clasp unlinks, and drops us deep and
down the dying ocean.
Daylight swift recedes.
The lamps come on.
The superstructure creaks, the engines whine.
There's none who care, who'll mourn us where we've gone,
Or save us from the crushing of the brine.

The Body

Philip Fracassi

The little girl next door hefted a dead dog as big as she was. Its matted mutt fur springy and clumped. Unkempt. Its eyes glass.

Lewis ignored them both. Pulled his detective badge and showed it to Blue Number One. Gave the street a once-over. Press van. A few open doors, black dots, abyssal gateways to unique despair.

BNO says the killer is likely nearby. Hiding. Perimeter wasn't breached.

I'd like to mustard gas the whole block just to be sure. Place was dead on its feet anyway. A boxer made of homes and melancholy swaying on its heels. One more punch should do it.

Inside, the body was laid out like a demon's sigil. Bent but oddly connected. A warning perhaps. Every bone broken, says Blue Number Two, who stood against a wall next to a spiky-haired blonde woman wearing medical gloves.

Lewis kneeled, donned his own latex fingers, poked the temple of the body's head. Eyes still open wide. Good. He'd ask for a detailed description of the ceiling when they drained the memory for playback.

He cocked his head like a dog, his knees beginning to ache from the couple stones he'd put on since the bombing a few years back had torn his wife and kids to pulpy mulch in their backyard. The grill was still half-in, half-out of the living room window. He liked the cold charcoal breeze that came through. Reminded him of happiness.

Typing. Someone was typing.

★★★

She pulled the sheet, too hard. The typewriter's barrel gave a short grating whine, still hungry. She fed it again, began beating keys like bad children. With a start, she twisted. The window was uncovered and full of backlit gray. An old hollow man, a neighbor she guessed, was staring in, holding a metal rake. The prongs tapped lightly against the glass.

★★★

The killer pulled up outside the house wearing bright yellow from head-to-toe. Scarf even. Contrasted the dirty-wash color of their world.

The little girl lifted a dead dog toward him and he smiled. Pet the thing.

Pet the dog, too.

★★★

Three miles away stood a corrupt cherry blossom tree. Fruitless. A rare blossom was plucked by a cold paintbrush stroke of wind and carried upward. Looking down, the blossom saw rooftops and smoke. Bodies prone on cobbled streets, laid out like signposts to hell. Cars the size of monstrous bread boxes whined for more speed on a cracked highway. The blossom soaked in radiation then keeled and fell, the breeze vaporized. There were no clouds in this city, not even sky. At mid-day you could see straight through to space itself. It was leaden and starless.

The blossom sank onto the mud shoulder of the river, inches from the current. It watched freedom and adventure roil past and wept.

★★★

The killer entered the house. Walked right past BNO and left riverbank mud footprints on the weary carpet. Lewis stood, knees snapping like fingers. The killer pulled a gun.

pop-pop-pop-pop

The sound of typing from the other room was so loud and insistent that BNT mistook the gunshots for keystrokes. The detective sprayed and spun, a graceful pirouette, and the red splattered like modern art, crimson poetry. A rare moment of beauty in a dead city. The spiky-haired blonde woman was transformed.

★★★

The novelist pulled the last sheet and rested it atop a stack of paper taller than a bowling ball. The epigraph was Frost regarding the heart's aching, the end of seasons. The hollow man with the rake was gone, replaced by a wall of cackling fire.

Later she'd go to the river and throw the words into it and watch them be carried far away.

Her story was not for this place.

Pamphlet to a Plastic Paradise

S.C.Burke

Release—RELEASE!

...explosives set off in a chain-reaction that turns night into day. Someone is up to no good and the entirety of society is being penalized for the crimes. A man, important to his own political cause, but essentially simple nobody, sits ablaze in the driver's seat of his automobile. This important nobody screams a staccato of sounds that ring out to a high pitch arpeggio and then it all settles with a charred whisper of death-scented smoke. The car-bomb has done its job—mission success. Until another key crunches through an ignition switch and—CLICK! KABOOM!—a mimicking cry from a different vehicle calls out to the world with a flare of fire, and another forgotten nobody whispers a hiss that forever burns hot. Somebody in the shadows has something to say and they're silently stating it in the loudest way imaginable. NOISE. FIRE. DEATH. Poetic, yet immediate and precise. Ermine eyes light up from the deep end of the abyssal alleyway, they watch the slow-motion dance of flames taking to fumes. The stranger smiles and smells the victory-smoke.

...explosions that sing against the somber night. Light in the world of Dark—breaking the laws of nature for a moment of mania. And then he moves onto the next. Laying against the greasy ground, plugging red wires where the blue should go and blue wires where the red should go—twisting them into a knot bundled and connected to a canister of gasoline lined in plastique-demolitions—*Semtex*. A poor man's car bomb. Low prep, high cost act of terror on ill-perceived important nobodies. Nihilism at its finest, hidden in plain sight.

Chapter Three, Page 86: an internet downloaded depiction blue-printing the engineering of bombs and explosives from everyday items found around the home. *Some assembly required.* He closes the book and trusts his instincts to take him through the final phases of the process.

Chapter Three, Page 88: an internet downloaded depiction of a bullet-proof vest modified with bricks of C-4 putty and a pressure-sensitive squeeze-bar. The anonymous bomber digs a hole, two foot by two foot deep, and creates a dead-drop location for acts that come later. He sees her hit the mark and hits speed-dial #0 on a burner phone—*SENDING...SENDING....* *SENT!* She looks like Marilyn Monroe as the pressure blows her skirt up around her chest and for a brief moment she tries to shove it back down, but it's too late, we've already witnessed her in all her prime, at her most vulnerable—in a mist of mystery liquids, miniscule pieces of Marilyn No-More, and burnt to a charred shadow of her former self on the ground she once stood so elegantly upon. Who was she? *Important.* Where was she from? *Unknown.* What was her name? *Unknown.* Who the fuck cares?

The stranger smiles and takes in the intoxicating aroma that infects the air around him.

Chapter Three, Page 90: fragmentation and irreparable wounding is explained in great depth, spanning an entire 36 pages of figures and examples. Moonshiner's mason-jar filled with rusty nails, BB's and razor blades floating in a reddish brown fluid that burns the skin on contact. Chemicals made from fertilizer, household chemicals and a little fuel. An IED that erupts with a vocal erosion that sings and sprays Bloody Violence out to the people, melting them into a mess of limbs and gurgling guts.

Stars speak loudly amongst the sky at night. Listen to the noise they make, as it carries a message. He can hear it—the NOISE that tells him to stalk the night with the same silence as the stars. *They burn so bright, down here in the streets, with the rest of us.* A chain-reaction of car-bomb blasts set in motion, minutes apart, like clockwork. Makeshift IED interrupts an entire city with shrapnel that shreds through every man, woman and child who stands in the line of fire. A false scene of self-immolation misleads evidence to show the monk was nothing more than a radical with a message that fell flat—an unsuccessful sacrificial suicide that was really a case of murder by a mysterious madman. A madman under the manipulation of a pamphlet-handbook he found at a crime scene of grisly murder in the name of a cosmic cult—the occult beat era that enlisted the manifestos of terrorism and arson, mixing them with the mysteries of murder amongst the cosmos.

Chapter Four, Page 132: the title of this chapter *Martyrdom in the Kingdom of Man*—a magnum opus that reveals the true path to becoming a real Martyr in the most primal sense of the word. Covering the history and politics that paint the act in absurdity and non-sense. Enlightenments towards the Universal beliefs of God as not a man, or entity, but pure energy that creates and destroys without the limitations of discrimination—no life, no death, no restriction of time or space, everything and nothing. The absolution of ABSOLUTELY!

The vessel we call our body is in fact a prison for the energy that is God in the truest form, thus I must free myself from that which restricts me from becoming what I truly am—a God. The Cowardly Creator and Great Destroyer of everything and nothing. I am timeless. Infinite. The sound that comes from silence. I am the NOISE!

A man with the plan to become a God in the most primal and Universal of senses—a Martyr in the Kingdom of Man. *Chapter Four, Page 213*: a step-by-step on how to execute a perfect act of Martyrdom in the modern era. *See Page 88*. He frantically flips back to Chapter Three and stares at the blueprint and the simplicity of his oversight. Simple human error—back to being transcended, a Martyr nearing the absolution of nothing, preparing for God status and paying attention to every step the book lays out. NOISE. FIRE. DEATH. DEFINITELY. INFINITELY. What began as a series of misled statements by a mystery man with a strange pamphlet has evolved into the ultimate act of terrorism and transcendence—Martyrdom—a word that has been torn asunder and redefined by radical movements, making the message about themselves and their personal beliefs in a fictional God who died before he really ever existed. *It's time to fulfill my role and become one with the cosmos. A true God—The Universe—Absolution of everything and nothing.*

...to cause harm to others, maiming them with wounds that were never really meant for the innocent, he turns his own flesh into a harness for the five needed components that come together to make an atypical IED. Filling his stomach with any form of combustible liquid, then sucking on methane to bloat the lungs and topping off his asshole with gasoline straight from the pump. Two birds with one stone—container and charge. Now a brutal and harrowing attempt to take out three birds with one stone—power source, fuse and activator switch. He meticulously feeds coils of copper and silver through his skin and into his veins, lining his entire insides to perfectly mimic the sketches in Grey's book of the human anatomy. His heart is a battery—assaulting and charging—a power source fused with silver and copper that is charged by the body's own electrical output—and at his fingertips is the completion of the final trifecta. The activator, fused into his fingertips.

Chapter Four, Final Page: Close your eyes. Inhale deep. Settle the nerves. And EXPLODE! He touches his hand to his heart, letting the senses in the tips of his fingers feel the flesh of what he used to be, one last time. And before anything can be seen, comes a creeping sense of finality in the form of a NOISE.

Release—Released!

...an explosion-aftermath of bloody and burnt papers.

Chapter Five, Page 303: taking the offensive on proper evidence maintenance—what should and shouldn't be left behind after your final act. Erase and eradicate any connection to your former life. This includes anything that may link you to your past identity; property, state appointed identifications, medical records, criminal background, and even ties to any friend or family members. You are simply known by your first name and you are entirely alone in this plain of existence. There are certified Disappearers who specialize in this field of work and are available for consultation upon request.

When the act is finished, essentially nothing should be left behind to prove you existed. However, it is important to properly identify yourself, by first name only, on all explosive devices. In the most recent string of explosive related incidents, it seems that they have tracked the Martyr back to his beginnings. Pieces of shrapnel, ball bearings, chunks of power suppliers, batteries, cellphone data chips, hunks of human flesh, they all wear the same name. The name of the culprit that is behind each and every one of these crimes against humanity, no matter the vessel, all evidence of evil inflicted wears the same name—

Suzie, After Hours

Konstantine Paradias

7 PM, Clocking in:

Omar loved singing to the meat, all nestled in its cold storage cradle.

From their perch up near the capsaicin pump, Omar and Istvan could see it writhe this way and that, its muscles pumping aimlessly as it tried to curl its wavy, layered mass into a ball. For a moment, it seemed as it if was trying to weave a makeshift hammock out of the miles of clear plastic tubing that ran out from the walls and stuck into its soft, pulpy mass. Istvan watched the toothless, drooling orifices open and close across the length of it, sucking in air as Omar gently lulled it to sleep.

"Sleep, sleep, little cumin flower" he sang, playfully "mama's breast's adrip with milk."

Istvan caught himself gently rapping his fingers over the pump, playfully tugging against the handle that kept the burning deluge at bay.

"Sleep, sleep, little cumin flower" Omar went on "papa left and mama's grieved."

"Whenever you're ready, Madame Superior," Vauhn's voice boomed from the walkie-talkie, breaking their reverie. Omar sighed, then motioned for Istvar to turn up the pump. The meat cooed softly, savoring a very private dream, oblivious to the brownish gunk that ran across the tubing and saturated its mass. It howled, uselessly, as the concentrated capsaicin suffused its pores and began to soak into the topmost layers, burning the tender muscle a muted blue.

"Sleep, sleep little cumin flower" Omar sang, his voice barely a whisper "strangers sleep in mama's bed."

Istvan turned the pump higher, sending ten billion Scoville units' worth of heat into the meat in three seconds flat. He watched the toothless, sucking orifices clamp shut as its simple pulmonary system shut down. He shuddered as the meat's muscles went into uncontrollable convulsions, its nervous system overwhelmed by the agony of a million ghost peppers flowing through its bloodstream.

"Sleep, sleep, little cumin flower," Omar managed, choking back tears "mama's gone and bought you bread."

"Alright, that should do it." Vauhn's voice came back on, as the meat finally went still. "Let's get cutting."

8 PM, Slogging in the Muck:

"You ever think that it's kind of inhumane?" Olga said, seven inches deep into a hunk of tenderloin. "What we're doing, I mean," she added. her filament saw hissed and the meat came loose and plopped down into the gore puddled on the stainless plasteel floor.

"Kinda doubt it," Istvan managed through clenched teeth, as he loaded the hunk on the whirring grav-cart.

"I mean, it's screaming, doesn't it? The meat?" Olga said, then began to hack away at another strip of tenderloin, cleaving across the length of its insides.

"That's just air rushing out." Istvan said, shooting worried glances at Omar, gently cutting at a loose joint. "Like, when you boil a lobster, you know?"

"What's a lobster?" Olga said, as she gently folded the strip of meat into a roll and plopped it into the cart.

"Big sea bugs. We had them before your time." Omar said, plopping his oversized shank onto the floor. Istvan watched the bit of meat writhe, its flesh knitting itself into a neat latticework of scars, closing off the wound.

"Was that before you guys invented the wheel?" Olga jeered. Omar shrugged and went right back to hacking at a dangling bit of stir-fry. "All I'm saying is, what if it *knows* what we're doing to it?"

"Oh I bet it does. It just can't do a damn thing about it." Istvan said, his eyes wandering over to the gently writhing bit of shank, at the languidly moving strips of meat piled into the cart. "Meat's got only enough brain to keep itself fresh; no spine to make itself move, no immune system to keep it safe from germs. It'd be as good as dead, the second it left storage."

"In here all day and a night, huh?" Olga said, as the superheated wire on her saw began to dice a hunk of meat, letting the cubes *plop, plop, plop* down into the sticky red muck. Istvan looked up, at the glistening wound on the ceiling, at the way it seemed to pucker up and writhe.

"Just like the rest of us." Omar said, not seeming to notice the way the stir-fry wriggled across his thick plastic gloves, how it seemed to coil itself around his arm before finally letting go, plopping down among the rest of its softly wriggling brethren.

Above them, the loin ceiling began to shake, dancing a spastic jig to the rhythm of a running saw. The skin-crews were already halfway through cutting the meat that had gone off, burnt off by the capsaicin OD they'd just given it. For a second, Istvan wondered if those bits wriggled, too. If the glistening wounds that the outside crews brought to light seemed half as eager as the harvest in his cart.

"Let's get a move on before some dumbass brings the gullet down on our heads." Omar said. Still looking up at the shuddering ceiling, Istvan swiveled his cart on its anti-grav port and headed up through the soft maze of veins.

10 PM, the Cheerful Giver:

Istvan watched as the red mass of pulpy meat ebbed gently behind a taut sheet of membrane. He ran the back of his gloved hand over it, tracing its smooth surface, the gentle contour of it and felt the soft throb of veins against his skin.

"Yo, Omar. I think we took a wrong turn." Istvan said. The old Iranian stopped, halfway through hacking at a congealed cascade of fat and turned to look at him.

"How's that?" Omar asked. Beside him, Olga scoffed and prepped her mince-drill, checking its jagged tip against the taut skin of tissue around her, revving up the motor with the pedal. "We went up the mesenteric, took a right into the first ileal, didn't we?"

"Then what the hell's a new heart doing here?" Istvan said, pointing at the bit of softly pulsing red. Omar shrugged and moved over to check, running his own gloved hands across the membrane. Behind them, Olga's mince-drill began to burrow into the soft mass of tissue, drilling a new, sucking wound, expelling freshly minced meat into the grav-cart.

"That's not a heart. We're too far off." Omar said, pointing up, to a place beyond the fillet ceiling, to the dark cavity beyond, where the pounding sound of two dozen pig-hearts, made giant and bloated by the miracle of science, beat in quaking synchronicity. "Besides, they never let us in the meat, not when they're growing a new one."

"Then what the hell is it?" Istvan shouted over the rising mechanical scream of the mince-drill filling the chamber. He could hear Olga's tool dig too deep, too hard. He heard the wet pitter-patter of chunks, filling up the cart and knew that he should stop her before she burnt out the engine.

"Can't know unless we look, right?" Omar said, removing his filament wire saw. With a single, seamless stroke, Omar slashed at the membrane, revealing the dark red thing beneath. It spilled out of its sheath, expanding outward like a cheap airbag, shedding blood and mucus as it went. Istvan grabbed Omar at the last second, dragging him out of its way, watching the flesh ripple out, bumping against the cart and knocking it over, spilling the pilfered meat down into the surface of the cave. Olga's mince-drill kept going, spattering chunks over the wall of dark red.

"Goddamn it, Olga, just quit the..." Istvan screamed over the howling of the mince-drill. It was naked noise now, unmuffled by the meat, a great machine roar that echoed inside the chamber. Omar said something that Istvan just couldn't make out. Slipping across the grime, Istvan pushed himself on his hands and knees and turned to shut the tool off.

The mince-drill had plopped free from the entry wound, leaving its engine running on the taut, soft floor. Omar babbled like a madman, endless groan of the engine. Crawling across the gore to dodge the wickedly-shaped head, Istvan reached down, found the power cord and twisted it, cutting it off from the cold fusion reactor nestled in the cart.

From his left, he could hear Omar bumbling in Kurdish, one word tumbling out of his lips again and again like a mantra. Again and again, the word came, like a schoolyard sing-song, like something ripped right out of a cockney children's book. Istvan's looked up, following the mince-drill's drop, across the trail it had made on the congealed gore on the surface of the meat, at the sucking flow of blood that came from an already healed entry-wound in the walls of the flesh chamber. There was a cancerous lump of scar tissue forming there, knitting itself into a bit of too-pale meat, weaving through a field of henna-red hair. A single, emerald-green eye stared of from the wound, before the flesh finally buried it in the blink of an eye.

Istvan jumped, as he noticed that the lump shuddered. He bit back his lip, to keep himself from screaming, when he noticed a small, rough hand push up against the thin layer of skin, uselessly trying to tear through it. Omar kept saying the word, over and over and Istvan knew the sing-song, had learned it by heart from a trid animated documentary he'd seen back in elementary school about human anatomy.

Liver, liver, cheerful giver...

The song went and Istvan jumped, as the mincemeat and the chunks from the cart began to slither across the floor, running across his wrists and legs, looking for purchase.

"Omar! Help me, goddamn it!" he screamed. Omar shot up from the surface, slipping on the gore. He choked, as a length of stir-fry wrapped around his throat and squeezed, so he slashed at it with his wire-saw, cutting a straight line into his cheek. Blood still flowing freely, Omar leaned down and started cutting away at the meat.

Around them, the walls began to contract and shudder. Above them, the surface crews began to scream. Somewhere, an alarm blared and the red corridor they were in shuddered violently, as the meat began to roll in its suspension tank, slamming against the clear plastic walls.

"It can take it! The meat can fucking well take it!" Istvan howled.

11 PM, Lockdown Tango:

Halfway up their way to the rectal artery, the meat finally stopped its thrashing. The screaming had stopped, twenty minutes ago. Outside, the facility alarms were still running, singing their pointless little dirge.

"Just up the next turn. That's all," Istvan panted, holding onto the arterial folds for purchase every step of the way. Omar was holding fast behind him, tethered to a line dangling from their belt hoops. "Just one more turn."

"She knows." Omar mumbled. "She's known what we've been doing to her, all this time."

"For Christ's sake, just shut up and help me."

"She's known the poisons we've been pumping in her. She's known we've been cutting into her. She's been prepping." Omar managed, breaking into a hearty little chuckle.

Istvan grabbed onto the line, tugged at it. Omar stumbled forward, slipping on the uneven footing, but didn't miss a beat.

"She's a clever girl, our Suzie." Omar said. Istvan winced at the sound of it, at the longing tones that Omar used, when he called the meat's name.

"It's not a *she*." Istvan said, digging his gloved hand deep into the soft flesh, tugging at it as he pulled both of them up the incline, slogging across the hundred feet leading up to the meat's rectum, out into the cold twilight of the storage locker. "It's just meat, Omar. It's just meat."

"So was Olga." Omar said and Istvan slammed his fist into his chest before he knew he was doing it. They tumbled down into the muck, bumped across the ridges, grappled at each other's pumpkin colored uniforms, snarled and struck at each other's exposed flesh. Istvan pinned Omar down, pushing his knees against his chest, crushing him until he was tired out, panting on the glistening surface.

"Get up. Get the hell up." Istvan panted, dragging Omar up the rectal artery, shoving him into the turn leading into the intestine. It bubbled and writhed, coated in a fine mince paste that frothed out through the sphincter.

"Sleep, sleep, little cumin flower" Omar sang through his cut lip "mama's left an empty bed."

Istvan grabbed Omar by his lapel, shoved him out of the sphincter. They tumbled across the meat's pockmarked fleshscape, through the shattered plastic pane. Newly-formed tendrils peeked out like ant larvae, wriggling in the air, caressing their overalls with their tiny, toothless mouths. From the corner of his eye, Istvan could see the tiny openings open and close in sync with the alarm's blare.

Awooooo they went, their tiny little voices rising up to the concrete ceiling. *Awooooo* they went, aching to bite into them and grab on and knit themselves around them, just like they did with Olga. Istvan crawled out of the jagged edges of plastic, walk-crawled up to the intercom station and bashed at the controls, screaming hoarsely at the receiver:

"Vauhn! This is Belly-Crew 3B, what the hell is going on?"

Istvan listened into the burst of static, leaning into the speaker as he tried to make sense out of the useless jumble of noise that came out in a steady stream. "Vauhn! This is Belly-Crew 3B, we got a woman down, we..."

"We're on lockdown." Vauhn's voice came, soft and desperate.

"Well, get a crew down here! Get headquarters! Tell them that we need someone to get us out of storage. Vauhn, the meat is out and it's growing, goddamnit!" Istvan said, barely keeping his voice in check.

"They know. No one's coming."

"What the hell are you talking about? We got the surface crews stuck down here, we got three dozen people..."

"Not anymore we don't." Vauhn said, cutting him off.

The receiver clattered down on the floor, as Istvan turned to check back at the meat. He saw the valley of bumps and tumorous ridges sticking out from the top of the meat, the writhing piles of scar tissue splayed out over what used to be fresh, glistening wounds. He watched the saws and drills clatter over the flesh, stuck inside tough scars that choked up their blades and flooded their motors. He saw a ridge of bone peeking out like a pale meridian line, its joints snapping into place. From his place of worship in the shadow of the meat, Omar laughed as he watched new muscles explode outward, testing themselves against the grip of gravity.

"We're way past acceptable losses. We're dead weight." Vauhn said.

Midnight, Growing Pains:

"There's always the runoff vent, " Omar offered. Istvan looked up at him, blinking away at the sweat running down his forehead. Storage had shut down air conditioning twenty minutes ago, leaving them to stew with the gasping, moaning meat.

"I'm not going down there," Istvan said, looking at the steady runoff that came pouring from the mass, dripping down from the shaking folds it had managed to drag out of the floor. The meat moved slowly, clumsily, like a baby taking its first steps. Sharp, hard things snapped into place inside it, making its muscles bulge. Istvan wondered how long it would be before it could stand upright.

"It's either that" Omar said, pointing at the drenched grate, the bits of hair and scalp sticking out across the grille. "Or you can wait for those feelers to reach you. They're getting closer."

Istvan looked at the wriggling, blind things, their snapping little mouths and could almost hear it now, over the muted din of the alarm, the gentle *click-clack, click-clack* of newly formed teeth. He wondered how the meat could ever have known to grow teeth, to make a spine and a liver. He wondered how a team of bioengineer kings would ever grow such a thing without making sure it could never fight back and then he realized that maybe, just maybe, the meat wasn't all pig or cow anymore. Maybe something had happened in there, a while ago. Some belly-shift bastard has slogged in there without the full gear or a supervisor had slipped down the wrong artery and the meat had gotten hold of him. Maybe, through him, it found out how to get out.

And maybe, just maybe, the only way for the meat to get out would be if it could get more like him. Enough for it to know exactly what it had to do to be free.

"We'll need a lever," Istvan offered, turning to the pile of assorted power tools, rifling through them and finally settling with ripping off an aluminum bar just barely hanging off the wall. Omar grasped the business end and led it down to the grate, sticking it against the opening of the grate.

"Okay, lean in," Omar said and Istvan put his weight behind the grate, watched as the metal began to badge, tearing away at the film of hair and gore, popping out of its place inch by inch. Above them, the meat growled as it hobbled on its stumpy legs. Thin, many-jointed things began to poke out of the wounds that grew across its belly, wriggling like baby fingers...

The grate popped out of its frame, letting a steady stream of gore and gunk splatter inside the runoff vent. For a moment, Istvan thought of Vauhn having a sudden, pointless heart attack for choking up the filters and laughed. He thought of corporate bigwigs going over their losses, thanking their lucky stars that the only people they lost were a bunch of illegal immigrants, all neatly absorbed into the meat, only to discover that a couple of survivors had irrevocably messed up their filtration systems in the process. He was about to share his private little joke with Omar, when he felt something snatching at his overalls.

"Omar! What the hell..." he turned, watching the tiny, jointed hand grasping at his work overalls, feeling tiny teeth biting into the fabric, ripping threads as they went. Halfway formed muscles tugged at him and he saw Omar backing away, as the meat kneeled down, testing the place behind him for another catch.

"Get. The grate," Omar whispered softly, reaching out with his gloved hand to poke at the tiny appendages that poked at Istvan's back. The fingers grabbed the material and began to rip away at it, tearing it free from the rest of his suit.

"Omar, what the hell are you doing?" Istvan managed, his voice barely above a whisper, his heart beating a machine-gun jig in his chest. Slowly, the arms let go, eagerly heading for Omar's exposed hand. Twirling this way and that, Omar began to slowly lead them away, tip-toeing across the gore.

Gritting his teeth, Istvan leaned harder into the lever, popping the grille free. Letting the lever clatter softly on the floor, he removed it and plopped down, into the ankle-deep offal. Above him, he could just barely see Omar moving out of sight, lingering over a sucking wound that grew along the length of the meat's belly.

"Sleep, sleep, little cumin flower" he sang, teasing "mama's breast's adrip with milk."

Istvan gasped the lip of the runoff shaft and pulled himself out so he could see. Omar was singing to the meat, dancing around its grasping arms, wriggling his fingers like playing with a baby. He cooed gently, wiping at the sweat that dripped from his brow in the sweltering heat, as he went on with his little song.

"Sleep, sleep, little cumin flower" Omar sang, as the wound above him opened up like a slit, exposing two perfect rows of pearly white teeth "papa left and mama's grieved."

Istvan struggled with the words, moaned like a kitten as he saw the glistening red tongue above Omar's head peak out through the meat's brand new lips, brimming with tendrils. He pointed up at Omar, but the man had already seen it, had felt it coming, even before the coarse, snapping tongue lapped at his overalls and tore them away in one single, smooth motion.

Istvan slipped into the shaft, biting his lip to keep from screaming. He took the first turn he could, heading into the narrow runoff shafts, slapping at the smooth concrete walls, straining to catch Omar's faint lullaby.

"Sleep, sleep, little cumin flower…" Omar went. There was a snapping sound, a sharp click and then the sharp, cracking sound, like chewing at week-old potato chips. It went on for a while.

1 AM, Movement:

Istvan listened to the softly growing sounds of the meat, as it burst into complex new forms, spattering chunks as it went, sending a flood of man-blood and mucus down into the filtration system, flooding the corridors.

He imagined its facade blooming like a cancerous orchid. He didn't move.

2 AM, Out:

Istvan felt the shudder, even though the thick plastic soles of his boots. He felt the meat above him slam into the stainless steel walls and reduce the concrete lining into powder with every successive jab.

"Omar, you dumb bastard," Istvan grumbled and moved, as his shelter began to shake in its foundations. He weaved across the corridors, following the vague, blinking directions of failing emergency lights up to an access ladder. A faint halogen glow seeped in from above. He supposed Vauhn wasn't all that spineless after all. That she had somehow managed to muster enough courage to break the rule and let some poor slob out.

The air of the control room floor was choked with the stench of something acrid and biting, the kind of smell Istvan knew from the old country. It was the reek of defeat, of offensives gone wrong. Of cocked guns discharging into their handlers. He didn't even need to turn his head to see that the top of Vauhn's head was gone, with the entry wound neatly dug into her palate.

She'd used a cattle bolt gun. The flat bolt-head was sticking out of the back of her skull.

Istvan looked the woman over: maybe if he'd ever seen her out of those coveralls, he might have found her beautiful. Maybe, when she out of the meat-farm, free to roam under the open sky, she wasn't choked with the night shift poison that she spat out from the intercom.

"You did good," Istvan said, before running his hands over her heavily made-up eyelids. For a moment, he thought about making her more comfortable, setting her head so the gaping exit wound wouldn't show against her matted black hair, but thought better of it. Vauhn had picked the easy way out.

The meat bellowed, its moan making the reinforced, shatter-proof glass of the control room judder in its frame. He saw it clumsily stand up, balancing its unwieldy weight on a half-dozen knees, a forest of hands reaching out of purchase. Something swelled and slowly pushed out from the top of its spine, a glistening half-globe infested with emerald green eyes. One of them pivoted in its socket, before fixing itself at the little creature in the overalls, just within its reach. In a split second, the meat pivoted clumsily and slammed itself against the control center, crashing into the metal. The pane of glass flew out of its frame and barely missed Istvan as he ducked for cover. When he looked up, he saw Vauhn's limp form, glued to the wall like a trapped butterfly, her beauty reduced into a smear.

Istvan rolled, as the meat stumbled and fell against the

control center, a newly formed mouth reaching its tongue out across the instruments, tearing levers and screens and panels apart as it whipped across the room. Fumbling with the emergency override, he manually undid the series of locks and stepped outside, into the processing floor.

3 AM, Suzie Wakes:

The processing floor reeked of leftover meat and blood that had gotten as thick as day-old jello, trapped in the guts of the processing machinery.

All around him, Istvan could see the husks of butcher-bots, idling over loin joints and steaks and lengths of intestine that had gone bad in a matter of hours, shriveling in the choking, stale air. The company had cut off climate control, had remotely unplugged their machines and had decided to wait the meat out, to let Suzie choke to death and go bad. Like him and everyone else in the graveyard shift, like every other bastard that had ever worked here, they still treated Suzie like a piece of meat.

"Right all along, you crazy bastard." Istvan muttered, barely holding back a chuckle. "You were right all along."

He grabbed at a butcher-bot and shoved it as hard as he could. The machine-worker stumbled on its spindly legs, teetered on the edge and finally fell down. It didn't even make a peep. No alarm blared. No supervisor came running down from their perch to throw the book at him. Istvan grinned and kicked at the robot some more, bent its chassis and stuck his hand in its guts, tearing away at hydraulic pumps to led the off-green lifeblood spill on the floor. The reek of oil rose up to join that of the rotting meat and Istvan barely held back from retching.

Beyond the reinforced door of the Storage floor, Suzie began to moan.

"Awwoooo" she went her voice a conglomeration of tiny howls that rose up from god knows where. Istvan listened in for Omar's barytone, for Olga's lilting voice, then stopped. That's not how he would choose to remember them. As meat, as bits in a bigger machine, as muscle and guts and blueprints for a brain.

"Shut up." he growled, against Suzie's mournful call.

"Awwwoooo" Suzie cried and Istvan grit his teeth, kicked at the assembly line so hard he felt his leg give. He fell to the floor, grasping his ankle, hoping he hadn't busted it. He felt his overalls get soaked in the hydraulic fluid, saw the rainbow patterns that rose up in the reflected halogen light and he knew.

Oh, he knew what he had to do to shut her up.

4 AM, Making Magic:

Warning: ProSqueak™ is not intended for human usage. Do not use ProSqueak™ as an antiseptic. ProSqueak™ is intended for usage as machine lubricant and anti-oxidization agent. Keep away from children. Certain flammability clauses may apply.

Istvan grinned at that last part. *Certain flammability clauses.* He shook the bottle with the blue cap, just to make sure. He couldn't quite make a bomb out of it, but he could start a fire. He knew it first hand, from back in the old country, when the shady little dealers that gave them guns to kill each other with would cut them off from the heavier-duty tools. Istvan tried to remember the name of the man who had taught him to make napalm out of brake fluid, but he couldn't remember anything past that awful chemical burn scar that had eaten away at half his cheek.

Counting the blue-capped bottles, Istvan found out he had about two dozen, squirreled away in an office cabinet. They used it here, whenever someone had a nasty cut or was headed for an infection. All you had to do was stick out your hand and your supervisor would soak the wound in the blue stuff. It would burn like a son of a bitch and you wouldn't be able to see straight for a week, but the wound would be squeaky clean. Besides, it was either that or calling an ambulance and having your ass thrown right out into the street.

Istvan carried the bottles down the stairs, toward the butcher-bot puddle. He ran the numbers in his head. From Storage, Suzie slammed at the walls and tore away at the bolted doors with clumsy baby-fingers the size of vespas. He ran to the Waste section and uncorked a barrel filled to the brim with guts, kicked it down and let it drain down into the runoff grate, watched it soak up the grille and pill out onto the floor. He grinned; the filters were done for.

With about a quart of offal left in the barrel, he rolled the rest back in the floor and emptied every last drop from every last blue-capped bottle in there. The leftover guts and guts sizzled and burned inside with a deep blue smoke. Good. That meant the stuff was working.

"Awwaaaaa" Suzie roared.

"Sure thing, sweetie. Sure thing." Istvan said, as he emptied every last drop inside the barrel, the began to gut the robots, tearing at the barrel and letting it all stew inside. The hissing stopped, replaced by a faint, bubbling noise, the kind that soda cans make after a good tumble down a flight of stairs.

"Awaaaa" Suzie said again, as she bent the reinforced steel and peeked inside with a single emerald-green eye. Istvan grinned.

"Awaaaaa" he moaned right back and laughed at the struggling little monster, at the processing floor, at the meat factory. He began to move the barrel away, to the edge of the floor, closer to the exit. His magic potion needed some time to stew and he had to make himself a solid fuse.

5 AM, Sticky, Sickly, Burning:

Istvan was dumping his final ingredient, a handful of cleaning powder, when Suzie moaned:

"Ouououout"

Istvan stopped, hand still caked with the cleaning flakes, feeling the chemical mix with the sweat in his palms. He shook his head, grit his teeth and rattled the barrel. The mix was thick and viscous. It had stopped bubbling. The colors had died down, muted inside it, leaving nothing but an ecru blob.

"Leeeet ouououout." Sizie howled and Istvan choked, staring up at the pudgy fingers ripping away at the wall, tearing apart the steel and concrete. A head peaked in, a glistening top that was infested with blinking eyes, a tongue that dangled uselessly down, lapping at the floor. Suzie was pushing her mass out of the hole, tearing herself at the jagged edges. Istvan looked for the bumps on her skin, the scar-tissue where the people he knew used to be and found that they were gone. Tufts of brown and black and auburn hair grew from Suzie's shoulders and back, infested with the tiny tendrils. Istvan turned to the side and vomited.

"Don't worry, sweetheart." Istvan said. "I'll let you out. I'll let us all out."

He stuffed the fuse into the barrel, wrung out of a sleeve from his coveralls and doused with pure ethanol, taken straight out of the machine shop. Reaching into his pocket, he took out a box of matches, the last little bit he had left from home. The sexy bunny-headed woman on the front winked at him and Istvan realized he didn't even know what she stood for anymore. The matches lit up and the flames licked at the rag, spread across the fuse. He kicked the barrel and watched it, as its lit end flopped toward Suzie's reaching fingers, as her tongue lapped at it and grabbed it.

"Ouououtt, Suzie sang, as she grasped at the barrel and held it close.

Then the napalm went in a flash of flame and smoke, dousing her. Istvan jumped to the side, just as a shard of hot metal struck the machinery, bounced and sank into his leg. He howled with her, screamed at the agony of feeling the searing metal cauterize the wound even as it tore into his muscle, watched Suzie's tongue shrivel as it choked on the flames, watched the meat and the tendrils and the heair burn away in layers off her, bit by bit, filling the processing floor.

Somewhere, a little bell began to ring. Sprinklers doused everything in a steady shower, but Istvan knew that his little bit of homeward magic wouldn't go out, not until it was good and done. Until it had turned the meat into char-broiled ashes. He imagined that even then, Suzie would flop around in the grey-black dirt, like something out of a horror film.

"Heeeeelll meeeee" Suzie screamed as she trashed around and crushed everything in her path. Istvan laughed, despite the agony in his leg, despite the pain and the choking smoke, even when the water pooled in his mouth and nearly choked him.

6 AM, Closing time:

The company sent some people in, to survey the damage and clean up the dead immigrant off the processing floor, to take some pictures to keep on file.

They didn't let the police in until they had cleaned up the bits of undigested bone that still lingered in the grey-black ash, until they had gotten rid of Vauhn's cattle bolt gun and had made damn sure they had chucked the night shift's personal items into the incinerator.

When the government and the WAT teams and the men in the hazmat suits came in, all they found was a dead length of tubesteak, burnt out due to a chemical fire. They also found the filters clogged and a steady stream of offal that had plopped into the ground water.

They found no camera feed of Suzie's rampage. They didn't ask about the gutted butcher-bots in the processing line. The company was so eager to see them off and deal with the PR nightmare that followed, that none of them bothered to check for the bits of marrow and tendons and stir-fry and loins that had fused together in the runoff shaft. No one believed the cleanup crew, who told them about the crawling bits of meat that had fled through the vents into the world beyond.

And in her dark little hiding place, swimming across the waste and the muck of the people above, Suzie savored her newfound freedom and sang, in her tiny, cartoonish voice:

"Sleep, sleep, little cumin flower, mama's breast's adrip with milk."

The Cottage

Tikuli

"Unlike many from the city I am no stranger to the whims of nature, but that day's sudden change of weather caught me unprepared. What started as a hike on a fair-weather day had suddenly been reduced to an ordeal. Winter totally changes perceptions of the land and no amount of off-season hiking could prepare me for the unexpected.

"Three unforeseen things happened that day. First, the weather suddenly turned nasty. Visibility rapidly decreased and the drop in temperature was rather sudden. Darkness shrouded the hills much earlier than usual and the crisp November air turned damp and cold. Second, I was forced to abandon my plan to return to the hotel because I twisted my ankle when my foot got caught in a thick root hidden by overgrown grass. Third, to my surprise, the cottage that I had discovered during one of my previous hikes, and where I was headed for shelter, was occupied.

"From previous visits I knew that the mist would have snaked through the network of paths crisscrossing the landscape, through the valleys and across the creeks until it curled around the cliff tops and canyons that were the mountains."

My class had been listening with rapt attention until one of the younger students gathered around the campfire broke the silence.

"I imagine it's great to explore somewhere that's not over familiar, so your twisted ankle and the worsening weather must have been very frustrating." He said.

"It was, the pain was excruciating and made it difficult for me to keep up my usual pace. I was on a steep path and I was breathless. I considered trying to find a vantage point from which to get my bearings, but realized that with the weather worsening, and with my throbbing foot, this wasn't going to be possible. Mist and darkness together can be terrifying especially when you're not prepared for it, but cold, wet, and with no other choice I had to go on.

"Even though I had visited the area before, my painful foot and the dense mist were disorientating, I'd strayed onto a nondescript trail that or might not take me towards the cottage. Dazed, confused and uncontrollably shivering I continued slowly through the mist, hoping that the path would eventually lead me to the cottage.

"Roosting birds in the woods had fallen silent and the sound-damping mist made the turbulent sound of the river down in the valley almost impossible to hear. It was obvious to me that, if ever I found my way to it, I would have to spend the night in the cottage no matter what, as my ankle continued to grow more painful with every step along the sloping and rock strewn trail. The forest was not very dense in this part of the hill, instead small and dense shrubs packed the landscape. The forest was not very dense on this part of the hill; instead small shrubs covered the ground.

"As I tripped over what I took to be a fallen branch, I yelled with pain but managed to get back onto my feet. Then I realized that this might be a blessing in disguise. I could use branch as a defence against snakes or other small animals I encountered. There were no big carnivores in this region, but even some small animals could inflict bad injuries. I hoped the cottage would not be too far away, as I was convinced I was heading in the right general direction, and despite the pain I tried to quicken my pace, as I was eager to reach my destination as quickly as possible.

"After walking for another ten or fifteen minutes, I finally saw the faint outline of the cottage not far ahead of me in the mist, and was glad that my choice of direction had been the right one. I remembered the area in front of the cottage with its overgrown bushes, which were now invisible. A rotten signboard dangled from a Pine tree close to the property. I recalled it used to have 'Hunter's Cottage' painted on it, two more tall pine trees stood on either side of the cottage porch. Outwardly the building appeared to be in good condition, and I thought it should provide good shelter for the night. I was surprised to see the dim glow of a lantern, indicating that someone was already in the cottage, but as I listened, I heard only silence. Whoever it was, unless they owned the cottage, must have forced the lock to open the door. As I approached, I saw a hazy silhouette on the porch."

"I waved and called out to her, for now I was sure that the silhouette was a woman. She remained silent, and stood so still that she might have been part of the structure.

"I drew close to the porch steps, and in the light from the lantern, I could finally see a face. I was surprised to learn that the figure was a woman.

Several students who had been staring silently into the flames looked up at the mention of the woman. "I had seldom seen an unaccompanied woman on those remote forest trails, and wondered if she had a companion in the cottage. I'd heard reports that many solo women hikers had gone missing in the mountains in the last few years. Though not superstitious I usually followed the advice of a former trek companion. 'Stay away from women while hiking. They're bad news,' he'd once said when we finally managed to part from a rather clingy and gabby girl during one of our hikes."

"That's not really true. Men have a habit of pointing fingers at women all the time. Not all women are clingy or gabby or bad news. Even men can be like that." Shyama, one of my female students, interrupted me with her strong voice. "Of course. My friend was generalizing—just as you are now, Shyama." The other students laughed and Shyama went quiet. Once the group had settled down again, I continued.

"I thought she was beautiful in an unconventional way. I hadn't realized that I was staring until she snapped her fingers in front of my face. I had even forgotten about my twisted ankle for a moment or two.

"I paused to light a cigarette, and watched for a moment as the smoke from my lungs rose and mingled with the smoke from the campfire. Some of my students stood to stretch their legs, and then reseated themselves in the circle of expectant faces.

"Mountains and forests can be both challenging and intimidating; we all need to be aware of the dangers involved in confronting nature head on.

"It was bone chillingly cold and the wind was picking up, but at least the rain had stopped. By then I was desperate for the comfort of a floor and four walls. I leant the branch I'd used as a support against the wooden railings of the porch, and then, as the woman stood back and opened the cottage door, I slowly made my way up the four steps and inside. As I passed her, I noticed the glow of her skin in the lantern-light and caught a faint scent of musk rose. Passing through the doorway, I saw that the lock had been broken. Inside, I shrugged my daypack onto the floor, and feeling more tired than I could remember ever having felt before, I limped to one of the plain wooden chairs and sat down for the first time since I'd stopped for lunch.

"Though she looked physically strong, I would never have expected her, or anyone else, to deliberately stand out in that piercing cold, it was almost as if she was expecting me—or expecting someone at least. When I looked back at her, instead of following me inside, she was still standing there, peering into the night.

"She was wearing warm pants and a hooded jacket. Her feet were covered in thick socks and her gloveless hands were wrapped around a tin mug. Inside the cottage her hiking boots lay near her backpack, along with a camera, some maps and binoculars. A lightweight sleeping bag lay open on the floor.

"I looked round when I heard movement on the porch, and then I watched her as she removed the lantern from its hook, turned, walked in and closed the door behind her. What a strange woman, I thought. She was observing me closely, but her silence was making me uncomfortable.

"I'm James Goddard," I said. As I extended my hand, I saw a smile flicker at the corners of her mouth, but it quickly vanished.

"She nodded and placed her mug and the lantern on a small wooden counter, then pointed to a pan,

"'There's some soup there if you want. You can sleep in there, take the lantern,'" she said as she pointed to a door at the back of the room. I smiled at her, watched her drag a chair to the open front to keep it closed, and regretted that I wouldn't be in her company for a while longer. I carried my daypack and lantern into the room, and then returned for the pan of soup. Only when I was in the room, with the door closed, did I realise that she hadn't told me her name. As I drank the cooled soup straight from the pan, it was filling but tasted of kerosene. I hadn't seen a stove in the cottage, so I guess she must have made it at a camp site and had somehow carried it with her. "I heard her settling down for the night. So, as quietly as I could, I spread a small wrap on the cot, then sat on the edge, removed my socks and boots and used an anti-inflammatory spray on my swollen ankle. A little later, my socks back on, I was stretched out on the rusted cot, trying to make myself comfortable for the night."

"'Maybe someone advised her to stay clear of men. Bad news, you know.'" Shyama muttered loud enough for me to hear. I ignored her and continued.

"During my hiking trips I'd heard a lot of weird tales around campfire, some true maybe, others folklore, but I'd never taken them seriously. Now, in the situation in which I found myself, thinking about the strange woman in the next room, those tales started to bother and amuse me at the same time.

"Lying on the cot I surveyed the tiny room. The walls were empty except for two large hooks on one side. My bed directly faced a window, and through it I saw the skeletal forms of winter trees limned with light that contrasted starkly with the cold, darkness of the night. Their branches were spread like the hands of the dead, bare, gnarled and chilling. As I watched, the branches curled into giant talons and scratched demandingly at the window.

"What I had seen was irrational, frightening, but turning on my side to avoid looking directly at the window, I tried to convince myself that it was nothing more than a product of my tired mind. In the dark, with my eyes closed, I thought about the mysterious woman. I heard her stirring, perhaps tossing and turning as she too tried to sleep. I must have dozed for a while, not real sleep, but that state between being awake and being deeply asleep, then

I was brought back to full wakefulness by a sound that's difficult to describe, whether it was coming from the main room, or was in my room, I couldn't tell. It wasn't like the sound of a person moving about, that would have caused the floorboards to creak, there was none of that, just the noise of something brushing across the floor. In the cold night, I shivered even more.

"As my sleeplessness dragged on, I distracted myself from the unexpected events and strange sounds of the night. In a sense, I felt trapped by the things that had occurred, it was almost as if my reality had been manipulated to take me to that place at that time. I forced myself to think about something else, and thoughts of my new life in a new apartment, in another city, another country, came to me. I had wanted to leave my meaningless life in cold and dreary England, it was sucking the spirit out of me. My increasing dissatisfaction had led me to accept an invitation to join an educational institute here in India, your college in fact, as a visiting faculty member. I thought about the people and places that I'd come to know when I had travelled in India, and the endless possibilities that awaited me in your busy, vibrant and colourful country. The hike was a last gift to me before I started my new job.

"At some point I must have drifted into real sleep, because a loud banging noise brought me fully and unwillingly awake. I got up from the cot as quickly as my swollen ankle would allow, and did my best to hurry through to the main room. The chair I had seen the woman move to act as a door stop, was back where it had been when I sat on it, the front door itself was swaying to and fro, and occasionally, as the morning breeze gusted, it slammed noisily into its frame. Through the window, through the swaying door, the room was flooded with light as the sun climbed above the trees. There was no sign of the woman hiker, whose presence had puzzled and perturbed me through the night. I hadn't heard her get up, pack and leave. I looked around, and apart from the mug still on the counter top and the scent of musk rose, there was no sign that she had been there at all. Where she had spread her sleeping bag on the floor, was a layer of fine dust that lifted and swirled a little in the draught from the door. The only footprints in the dust, I knew, were from my own hiking boots, and there was nothing to show that anything had softly trodden that floor, as I am still convinced I'd heard in the night.

"With a chill running up and down my spine, a feeling of dread, of not understanding, I went back to my room, dressed for a day on the trail, and packed my things. As I did this, the window flew suddenly open, filling the room with the cool, sweet, pine scented morning breeze. I looked up and saw the pine trees gently swaying. Feeling an urgent need to leave that place I lifted my daypack onto my shoulders, hurried from the cottage with a palpable sense of dread, collected the branch I had used as a support, and taking the same path by which I'd arrived, headed away as quickly as my sprained ankle would allow. Every rustling leaf, every animal sound, quickened my pulse as, with a palpable sense of dread, I moved away from the cottage. I wanted to be out of that forest as quickly as possible, and I hoped I would never have to return there."

I stopped and glanced at the faces of my students, now lit only by the dying glow of our campfire. They had been listening to me in rapt silence.

"Oh my God, the woman was a ghost. The local tales weren't crap after all." One of the boys said quietly, as he huddled closer to his companions.

In the tiger reserve around us, I could hear animals moving, but there were no alarm calls announcing that a big cat was on the prowl.

"Is that what you think?" I asked rhetorically as I raked the dying embers with a stick. "Does anyone else have a theory?"

The group muttered quietly among themselves, as I smiled and wondered if even one of them would understand.

"No, not the woman. The trees." A girl called out suddenly. Immediately the others demurred, so I let them argue for a while, until it was time to turn in for the night.

"Are you going to tell us?" Someone asked.

"Think about the story I told you, consider the evidence, then you'll realise that only the trees could have been what was haunting that place."

Be Quiet

Dale P. McMullen

Man, I've messed up.

Two years in prison or a year here, that was my choice—and I've made the wrong one. How hard could being a silent monk be I thought. This is the governments new thing, send criminals off to learn the values of inner peace, come back a year later a changed man. It made sense on a lot of levels; it cost them pennies to run it, you get criminals shipped away (out of sight, out of mind), you run a success story on the news every now and again and everyone is happy. Now don't get me wrong, I think this works for the majority of people, I just hate it. I was shipped to The Holy Isle just off Arran.

As I was saying, I've been here now for about nine months, I think. There are no communications with the outside world, no TV or newspapers, no letters. I have no idea how my wife is, she could have been hit by a car months ago for all I know, surely they would tell me that? Wouldn't they? All I know it was freezing when I got here and now it's sunny. I make that about July. I have been living a routine of daily meditation, rice and readings. It's not this that's driving me mad, I need to talk, I have always talked, even when it was inappropriate, I talked. I can't stand the silence. So why don't I talk you ask? Because I can't. I've been fitted with a device, if I talk, if I make a sound, a month will be added to my sentence, I've learned to sneeze and even cough silently, I can't be here for any longer than I need to be. I need to get home to her, I need to make sure she's okay.

Now that I am coming toward the end of my sentence I will have interviews to see if I am ready to be returned to the outside. Today is my first one, I sit at a small desk with a small screen in-front of me, no bigger than seven inches. A young woman sits across the desk from me, she's the first woman I have seen here, she's beautiful. Long brunette hair swept back, official looking thick rimmed glasses frame her face. She crosses her legs with her clipboard resting on her lap. She begins.

"I'm here to conduct your good behaviour interview, the monks have reported that you have been a model prisoner and because of this you have been granted this interview. You will have the opportunity to ask one of the pre-selected questions shown in-front of you. This is also how you'll answer my questions. There will be pre-selected answers shown on-screen and you simply select one. I ask you to remember that your vow of silence is still in effect and speaking shall be punished by a further month of incarceration. Do you understand?"

The screen separates into two, a white background with the words YES and NO are displayed so big that it's almost comical. I select yes, it makes a beep—and the words disappear.

"Excellent. Now I will continue. Now please, stay relaxed, this is just an informal review to see how you're getting on." She clears her throat and shifts in her chair, smiles then resumes.

"Do you feel that you have learned from your time here?"

I select YES. A further two boxes now appear.

I ENJOY BEING A MONK AND WOULD LIKE TO CONTINUE WITH MY LESSONS

I FEEL LIKE I AM READY TO RETURN HOME

I select the second option.

"So, have you enjoyed your time here?" She's scribbling down a lot of information.

YES

NO

I select yes, even though it's a complete lie. I just know what these guys want to hear, "I'm better now I promise" blah blah blah.

"So why don't you want to stay if you're enjoying yourself?"

I FEEL I HAVE LEARNED ENOUGH

I COULD LEARN MORE

I select the first one.

"And what would you say you have learned?"

I HAVE LEARNED INNER PEACE

I HAVE LEARNED THAT I WANT TO GO HOME

I have learned inner peace.

"—and do you have any feelings of resentment toward the court for your sentencing?"

YES

NO

Of course I do, I fucking hate this place. I select no.

"OK, I have to admit I am getting slightly confused. You enjoy staying here but want to go home. You want to go home and yet you are not angry about being sent here. I don't mind telling you that I would be angry about being here. I would not want to be here at all. Frankly, I feel like you aren't answering my questions honestly. I ask you to please relax, and please answer these questions to the best of your ability." She smiles and bounces back up to a fully upright position on her chair -man she's gorgeous—I take a long blink to regain my composure.

I go back to the questions. Do you feel like your sentence of a year is long enough, too long or not long enough.

The three options appear, I select long enough.

"Do you think you'll continue your practises when you get home?"

NO

MAYBE

I honestly select maybe.

"Could you elaborate?"

I MAY CONTINUE WITH PRAYER

I MAY CONTINUE WITH MEDITATION

I MAY CONTINUE MY VOW OF SILENCE

I MAY CONTINUE WITH MY READINGS

I select I may continue with meditation. If I take anything away with me it would be that, it's the only thing that has got me through this.

"Do you have any feelings of frustration?"

YES

NO

I select yes.

"Do any of these options apply?"

SEXUAL

IGNORANCE

FOOD

BOREDOM

I think all would apply here, I didn't realise I was sexually frustrated until I saw her today—I haven't had sex in nearly a year! Ignorance, I guess this means I have no idea what is going on in the world, with my family, friends and everything else in-between. The food is shit and I'm getting a bit bored of this fucking interview. I do however: select ignorance.

"Yes, that would be the most common answer, although I do have to admit sexual frustration is a close second. Do you feel sexually frustrated?"

I select yes.

"I understand, now how do these options apply."

I AM SLIGHTLY SEXUALLY FRUSTRATED

I WANT SEX NOW

I select the slightly one without looking at her, although I can feel her looking at me.

"And if you were to be offered sex now would you take it?"

YES

NO

I select no quickly. Further options open up.

I AM MARRIED

I DON'T HAVE THE URGE

I HAVE NO FEELINGS ON THE MATTER

I instinctively say I am married, like all married men do.

"Thank you, I know that is an awkward part of the interview. We have to cover it, there are a lot of sex criminals to process, so we just cover everyone." She flips a page on her clipboard.

"Okay we are now coming towards the end of our first interview, I see it as a success and I will be conducting more with you from now until your release. How do you feel it went. 1 being bad 5 being the best."

The numbers 1 through to 5 appear on a horizontal line on screen. I hit 4, I have no idea how it went really, I'm just a bit confused.

"Brilliant, glad you agree. Now you have the opportunity to ask me a question."

WHEN WILL I BE RELEASED?

WHAT IS TODAY'S NEWS?

HOW IS MY FAMILY?

CAN I BE MOVED TO ANOTHER HOLDING MONASTERY?

Without thinking about it I ask how my family is. Is she OK? I need to know. I look at her desperately for news. She notices my answer and flicks slowly through her papers. I sit forward with anticipation, my stomach fills with nerves.

"Family, family... Ah! Here we are. Your mother and father are in good health and still in the same home. Your brother has had a son, they named him Shaun. The baby is in good health. Congratulations!" She looks up from her sheet smiling. She nods. Wait, is that it? What about my wife? She clearly notices my face and looks confused back at me. I panic and blurt out.

"My wife!?" I give myself a fright, I didn't mean to speak, it just happened. I don't even sound like myself. My collar bleeps, shit.

"Sorry, this is all the information I have. I'm sure it's just a clerical error. I'm disappointed you spoke, just as the interview was coming to an end. I'm afraid your collar logged that."

I open my mouth to plead my case but think better of it and just slump in my chair.

"Please don't be disheartened, most people slip-up two or three times. I look forward to our next session. Hopefully I'll have some answers for you then."

I don't know how long ago that interview was, months at least. Now I lie awake every night in silence. I'm starting to forget what my wife looks like. I've learned to cry silently.

Dark Fence

Matt Bialer

4, 256 satellites in orbit

But there is one

That has been

In orbit the longest

And nobody knows

Who launched it

Nobody knows

Appears some nights

Some nights it doesn't

Black Knight Satellite

An oracle in the sky

Black Knight Satellite

Appears some nights

Some nights it doesn't

My business partner Brad

And I are obsessed

We think it exists

It exists

By day we own

GEEKS ON CALL
Computer Repair

Click me to talk
To a Geek

Send people
To your home

To do
This sort of thing

Kind of like
A plumber

For a computer

GEEKS ON CALL

But in our off hours

Down time

Talk about how certain we are

How certain we are

That it exists

It exists

Black Knight Satellite

An oracle in the sky

Brad—
Skinny
Dark hair
Unshaven
Specs
An earring

A geek

His pot of coffee

We need more information dude

What are you doing?

We need to hack the Pentagon

You're crazy
You'll land us in jail

He's also a part time hacker

Goes by handle
TheRighteousOne

Mostly just mischief

Corporations or institutions
He can't stand

TheRighteousOne

On the phone
With Verizon

Posing as a Verizon worker

We have a customer
On scheduled call back

I'm unable
To access

Customer data base on my own

My tools are down

4, 256 satellites in orbit

But there is one

That has been

In orbit the longest

And nobody knows

Who launched it

Nobody knows

My tools are down

Up there
In plain sight

But invisible

A shadow

Orbiting the Earth

Oblong shadow

In 1927
Jorgen Hals

Civil engineer
In Oslo

Uses early commercial
Radio receiver

To listen

To shortwave transmission

From a station
In Eindhoven

Notices something
Extremely odd

Signals
Being reflected back

By something

Echoes

At irregular intervals

Echoes

Sometimes 3 seconds
Sometimes 15

Hals unknowingly discovers
LDEs

Long Delayed Echoes

A shadow
Orbiting the Earth

Oblong shadow

Appears some nights

Some nights it doesn't

Brad still on the phone
With Verizon

Gives them
Fabricated employee V-code

Unique code
Verizon assigns employees

So they can obtain
Information they are seeking

From out in the field

Seeks an account number

Four digit PIN

Back up mobile number
On the account

A Gmail address

Last 4 digits on a bank card

What the hell
Are you doing Brad?

What are you doing?

Shhh!

My tools are down

Echoes

At irregular intervals

Echoes

Sometimes 3 seconds
Sometimes 15

LDEs

Long Delayed Echoes

So intrigues scientists

Huge experiments conducted

Into the phenomenon

Echoes are real

But nobody has an idea

What is causing them

No idea

My tools are down

Oblong shadow

1954
An incredible story

Appears in
AVIATION WEEK AND SPACE TECHNOLOGY

A mysterious satellite

In Earth's orbit

A mysterious satellite

Before we even have satellites

The Pentagon is furious

Do not want the discovery

To be made public

Appears some nights

Some nights it doesn't

Black Knight Satellite

Not to be made public

My tools are down

An oracle in the sky

A shadow

Orbiting the Earth

**Click me
To talk to a Geek**

Echoes are real

An explanation
Is put out

An explanation

Satellite

Is actually an asteroid

Just an asteroid

While it's possible
For Earth's orbit

To capture
An asteroid

Extremely unlikely

Rumors
That it's artificial

Artificial

Brad's on the phone
With Google

I've been locked
Out of my account

Ask security questions

Last four digits
Of his bank card

Name and phone number
Associated with account

All of which he has
From Verizon

Reset password

You're going to get us arrested Brad

You know that

And don't do it
From our office devices

I always tell you that
You never listen

Dude, it's cool

I'm trying to
Dig up the truth

I'm a whistle blower

A whistle blower

Just an asteroid

My tools are down

Click me
To Talk to a Geek

4,256 satellites in orbit

But there is one

That has been

In orbit the longest

And nobody knows

Who launched it

Nobody knows

Echoes are real

I've been locked
Out of my account

My phone rings

It's my wife

I can't find Claire

She not answering my texts

Turned off
Locator on her phone

Our 15 year old daughter

Only child

Good kid
Good student

But she's been pushing back lately

Pushing back

Fiery red hair
Like her mother

Likes her Swedish fashion
From H & M

Satin tops
With ruffled sleeves

Super skinny low jeans

Bomber jackets

And she is
A girl who codes

Summer immersion program

Learn HTML, CSS
Java Script

Coded an mp3 player

When I learned
I could use code

To make something
I use everyday

Makes me braver Daddy

A girl who codes

Echoes are real

I can't find Claire

Not answering her text

Finally she answers one of mine

What are your plans?

Hanging out with PPL

Don't be home too late

No reply

And she is
A girl who codes

Summer immersion program

Learn HTML, CSS
Java script

Codes an mp3 player

When I learned
I could use code

To make something I use everyday

Makes me braver Dad

A girl who codes

Echoes are real

I can't find Claire

Not answering her text

Always on her phone

Texting

Snapchat

Instagram

Chat rooms

Giggling

Using their slang

Oh word

Oh, really?

Lit

Fun

Ode ppl here

A lot of people here

You are being mad annoying Daddy

Facts

I agree

Facts, Daddy

We're worried

About the apps she uses

DM on Instagram

Can't verify

The identities

Of the sender

Very popular app

For kids under 18

Also popular

With sexual predators

Creepy older men
Can slide into your DMs

Be careful Claire

Be careful

My wife heard her

Tell a friend

About a boy

She met

In this app

If it's even a boy

She's worried

I am too

We don't know
Who he is

And now

Her phone

Is an impenetrable fortress

Impenetrable

Hidden apps

Vaulty

Password protected app

Media
Such as videos and photos

Can be hidden

From main image gallery

Won't take it off

Or tell us the password

You are being mad annoying!

It's fine

Facts, Daddy

We should confiscate

Confiscate the phone

I think she has an online boyfriend

We don't know who he is

Is an impenetrable fortress

Dude, either take the phone away

Or hack into it

You got no choice

A girl who codes

I can't do that

Oh yes you can

Can't verify

Why don't we do something as a family?

Go to a museum

A movie

Echoes are real

I've been locked
Out of my account

Up there
In plain sight

But invisible

A shadow
Orbiting the Earth

Oblong shadow

Appears some nights

Some nights it doesn't

Have the Soviets

Managed to secretly

Get something
Into orbit

3 years before Sputnik

First publically acknowledged satellite?

Or is the object

Something from further afield

Further afield

Can be hidden

From main image gallery

Won't take it off

Or tell us the password

Can't verify

Facts, Daddy

My tools are down

1957

The Soviets launch
Sputnik 1

First manmade object
To be launched

Into Earth's orbit

Object is tracked

Shadowing Sputnik 1

Shadowing

Two months later
Launch of Sputnik 2

Carrying a passenger
Small dog named Laika

But it also

Has a mysterious follower

Tracked in space

By an object

Neither the Soviets
Or Americans

Have any idea

Of what it is

Any idea

Dr. Luis Corrralos

Communication Ministry
In Venezuela

Photographs the object

While taking pictures

Of Sputnik 2
Passing over Caracas

In polar orbit

Which is not possible
At this time

Polar orbit

What is it?

What is it?

Long Delayed Echoes

Sometimes 3 seconds
Sometimes 15

4,256 satellites in orbit

But there is one

That has been

In orbit the longest

And nobody knows

Who launched it

Nobody knows

Something from further afield

Further afield

Can be hidden

From main image gallery

Won't take it off

Or tell us the password

Can't verify

Facts, Daddy

Appears some nights
Some nights it doesn't

An oracle in the sky

My tools are down

Click me
To Talk to a Geek

Brad is typing furiously

What are you doing Brad?

What are you doing?

Getting closer to the truth Dude

You're hacking the Pentagon

Not on our devices

Maybe
Maybe not

Brad, you're going to get us arrested

You're nuts

Chill Dude I've done it before

Nobody knows

Who launched it

Nobody knows

Won't take it off

Or tell us the password

Can't verify

I sent you a little app I designed

Yeah?

I named it Hawkeye

You can hack
Into Claire's phone

See what she does

The photos

Who she's texting

Break into the impenetrable fortress

It's the bunker buster

The bunker buster

Oh no
I couldn't do that

Yes you can
And you will

A girl who codes

Why don't we do something as a family?

Go to a museum

A movie

Echoes are real

Hacked the Pentagon

Has a mysterious follower

Tracked in space

By an object

Long Delayed Echoes

1960

Dark Fence

A kind of radar trip wire

Stretches across

Width of United States

Designed by Naval Research Laboratory

Keep track

Of satellites

Whose radios

Are silent

Dark Fence

Huge transmitters

Established
At Gila River

Near Phoenix, Arizona

And Jordan Lake,
Alabama

Spraying radio waves

Upward

In the shape of open fans

Picking up signals
That bounce off

Any object
That pass through the fans

The Commanding Officer
Of Dark Fence

Decides that something

Is circling overhead

Roughly polar orbit

Races to the Pentagon
In person

To report
Menacing stranger

The US does not know
What is going on

Over its own head

Large black object
In polar orbit

Around the Earth

Possibly weighing
As much as 15 tons

Particularly odd

Neither the US
Or the Soviets

Have the ability

To put an object

In 1960

And the purported weight

Far beyond

What either country

Capable of getting into space

Far beyond

My tools are down

Press reports

Cause major splash

With the public

Time Magazine

Newsweek

Pentagon quickly
Steps in

To kill the story

Derelict remains

Of Discoverer satellite

Gone astray

Just space debris

Cannot verify

I've been locked
Out of my account

Just an asteroid

Echoes are real

An oracle in the sky

A shadow

Orbiting the Earth

Oblong shadow

Facts, Daddy

But the explanation

Does not convince many

Does not convince

Whatever it is
In Earth's orbit

Acquires a name

Black Knight Satellite

Appears some nights

Some nights it doesn't

Black Knight Satellite

An oracle in the sky

**Click me
To Talk to a Geek**

Brad still
Furiously typing

What are you doing?
I told you to stop

Not from our equipment

Sorting through files
Of the Pentagon

TheRighteousOne

Did you use the app yet?
Did you use Hawkeye?

Not yet
I feel funny

A girl who codes

You got to know what's going on dude

Hmm I can't but feel
That our Black Knight

Is tied to Ghost Fliers

There you go again
With Ghost Fliers

They're not related Brad

Ghost Fliers

The first report comes in
September, 1933

Northern Sweden

The reports coming in

"Like drops in a rainstorm"

Neither blizzards

Nor fog

Appear to hamper

These ghostly aircraft

What are they doing

Up in a region

With few aircraft

Able to fly through anything

A shiny bright light

Just like a blow torch

8 engines
Carrying pontoons

Winging its way

Through line of mountain valley

Flying very low
With powerful searchlights

February 2, 1934

Parliamentary debate

About the Ghost Fliers

Swedish Prime Minister

Declares it's not yet proven
That the Ghost Fliers exist

Absolutely no reason
To take any action

But the sightings continue

96 unexplained

But confirmed sightings

Until February 23, 1934

Secret committee formed

To investigate the Ghost Flyer phenomenon

Codenamed Project Searchlight

Swedish Air Force

Deploys reconnaissance airplanes

For 3 months

Patrol Northern Sweden

Patrols also out on skis

To different mountains

To man the 34 inch searchlights

Mounted on the peaks

Searchlights bathe the darkness

Bathe the darkness

But find nothing

It's related

I feel it in my gut dude

It's not related

Up there
In plain sight

But invisible

A shadow
Orbiting the Earth

Oblong shadow

Appears some nights

Some nights it doesn't

Just space debris

Gone astray

Cannot verify

I've been locked
Out of my account

Just an asteroid

Echoes are real

Facts, Daddy

May 15, 1963

Gordon Cooper

Launched into space

Last Gemini mission

Orbits Earth 22 times

34 hours

19 minutes

49 seconds

546, 267 miles

Reports seeing an object

Near his craft

Glows

With a greenish hue

Glows

Back on Earth

Object seen

By dozens of witnesses

On the radar screen

Of NASA's
Muchea Tracking Station

In Australia

News widely reported

In the press

But NASA's reaction
Is odd

Forbid reporters
From asking Cooper

About the object

Put out a story

That carbon monoxide leaked
In the capsule

Caused Cooper
To hallucinate the sighting

Ghost Fliers

Searchlights bathe the darkness

Bathe the darkness

Nobody knows

Who launched it

Nobody knows

Won't take it off

Or tell us the password

Can't verify

Appears some nights

Some nights it doesn't

I'm in Claire's DM

Selfies

Pouting
With beads

Photos of her friends

Selfies with friends

Food

Crepe with Nutella

Avocado spread

An exchange with someone

Hashtag: **Friendly Ghost**

what do you like to do?

idk music netflix tech stuff

what do you like?

**music video games partying
r u into going to stuff like that**

idk I guess

Can we chill

idk your real name
or where you live tho

is that a yes

maybe but not
until I know who you are

Friendly Ghost

Can't verify

The identities

Of the sender

Very popular app
For kids under 18

*Creepy older men
Can slide into your DMs*

Should I tell her Mom?

hould I tell her
That I'm spying?

Echoes are real

Black Knight Satellite

An oracle in the sky

4, 256 satellites in orbit

But there is one

That has been

In orbit the longest

And nobody knows

Who launched it

Nobody knows

My tools are down

Up there
In plain sight

But invisible

A shadow

Orbiting the Earth

Oblong shadow

Facts, Daddy

**Click me
To Talk to a Geek**

In 1972

Scottish astronomer
Duncan Lunan

Studies the LDEs

Long Delayed Echoes

From 1927
In Oslo

Echoes

At irregular intervals

Echoes

Finds that
Varying delays

Shown in echoes

When mapped

On a graph

Forms a map

Of Epilson Bootes star system

Deciphers a message

A message

Our home is Epilson Bootis
Which is a double star
We live in the 6th planet
Of 7
Our 6th planet
Has 1 moon
Our 4th planet has 3
Our 1st and 3rd planets
Each have 1
Our probe is in
The orbit of your moon
This updates the portion
Of Arcturus
Shown in our maps

Lunan has a hunch

The graph he creates

Matches how

Epilson Bootis

Looked 13,000 years ago

Black Knight Satellite

From a distant star system

Orbiting the Earth
Since prehistory

Prehistory

But then Lunan

Very suddenly
Changes his mind

It's not a map
I was wrong

It's not a map

A shiny bright light

Just like a blow torch

Echoes are real

A shadow
Orbiting the Earth

Oblong shadow

Appears some night

Some nights it doesn't

A girl who codes

Facts, Daddy

Should I tell her
That I'm spying?

Why don't we do something as a family?

Go to a museum

A movie

Tonight

Claire comes with us

To see the movie
Hidden Figures

Based on a true story

A team of African American women
Provide NASA

With important mathematical data
To launch the program's

First successful space program

3 black women
Who work in NASA's computer section

In 1961

They are the computers

Drink from a pot
Of coffee

Labeled "Colored"

Walk 20 minutes each way

To a building
Where nearest restroom

For black females is located

Katherine works out

The hidden figures

Needed for
John Glenn's mission

They are the computers

Yes, they let women
Do some things at NASA Mr. Johnson

And it's not because
We wear skirts

It's because we wear glasses

Have a good day

Claire exhilarated

That's my favorite movie!

I want to be like Katherine
She's so inspiring

At work next day

Brad still furiously typing

Now look at this dude

High resolution photos

Very detailed

Filed labeled: **BLACK KNIGHT OBJECT**

Space Shuttle Endeavor
1998

Some photos were released

But not like these

Not like these

Look at it dude

So ancient looking

They said it
Was a lost thermal blanket

From the International Space Station

That ain't no blanket

I'm trying to use
The Hawkeye app

But it's not working

It's not working

Can't get in

Dude you've been punked!

A girl who codes

I've been locked
Out of my account

The lights in the room flicker

And go off

Our computer screens

And phones light up

Wide, expanding

Room opening light

Five Haikus For a Friend

JS Breukelaar

Walking the High Line,
talking words, and worlds remade
Home stays on the page.

★★★

"Spectre No. 1":
White Cities turn a blind eye,
black-inked cobble-stones.

★★★

Parisian Jew, displaced,
he bangs out silence
with a hollow leg.

★★★

Tyrannically,
distance modifies its lie:
"Real punks never die."

★★★

Bills to pay,
and all—in anyway,
he wagers and rages alone.

www.ingramcontent.com/pod-product-compliance
Lightning Source LLC
Chambersburg PA
CBHW031211260626
47169CB00007B/2018